MW00757020

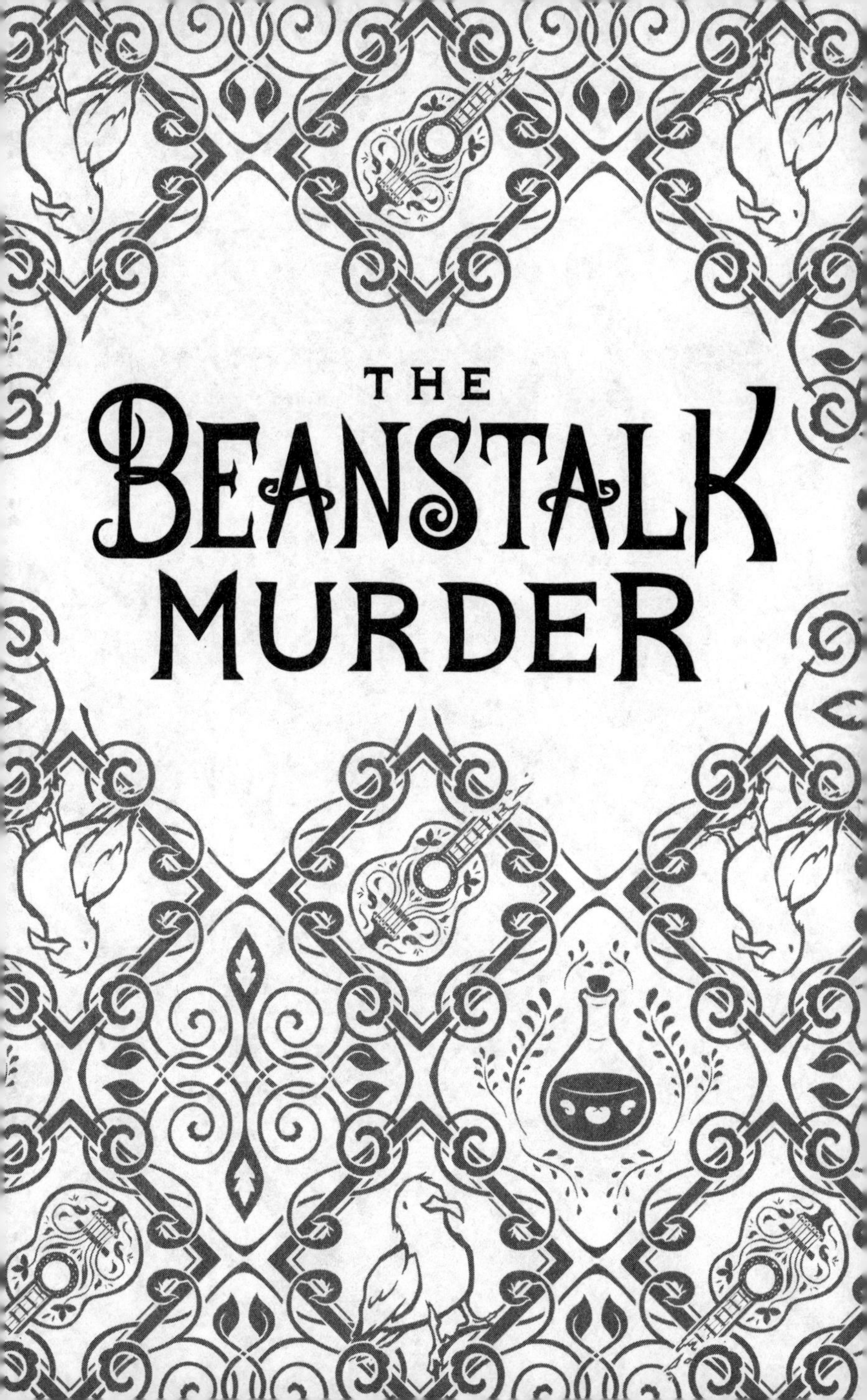

THE
BEANSTALK
MURDER

The Beanstalk Murder

P. G. Bell

FEIWEL AND FRIENDS
NEW YORK

A Feiwel and Friends Book
An imprint of Macmillan Publishing Group, LLC
120 Broadway, New York, NY 10271 • mackids.com

Library of Congress Cataloging-in-Publication Data

Names: Bell, P. G. (Peter Gwilym), author.
Title: The beanstalk murder / P.G. Bell.
Description: First edition. | New York : Feiwel and Friends, 2024. | Audience: Ages 10–14. | Audience: Grades 7–9. |
Summary: Eleven-year-old Meadow Witch apprentice Anwen Sedge, along with her grandmother and rival Cerys, find themselves in the Sky Kingdom with giants after a dead king falls onto their rural village, prompting them to solve the mystery of the king's death before they can return home.
Identifiers: LCCN 2023045644 |
ISBN 9781250864840 (hardcover)
Subjects: CYAC: Fantasy. | Witches—Fiction. | Giants—Fiction. | Mystery and detective stories. | LCGFT: Detective and mystery fiction. | Fantasy fiction. | Novels.
Classification: LCC PZ7.1.B45234 Be 2024 | DDC [Fic]—dc23
LC record available at https://lccn.loc.gov/2023045644

First edition, 2024
Book design by Meg Sayre
Illustrations by Jordan Kincaid and Meg Sayre
Feiwel and Friends logo designed by Filomena Tuosto
Printed in the United States of America by Lakeside Book Company, Harrisonburg, Virginia

ISBN 978-1-250-86482-6 (paperback)
1 3 5 7 9 10 8 6 4 2

ISBN 978-1-250-86484-0 (hardcover)
1 3 5 7 9 10 8 6 4 2

For Mum & Dad,
who always fed me books,
and never laughed when I said
I wanted to write my own

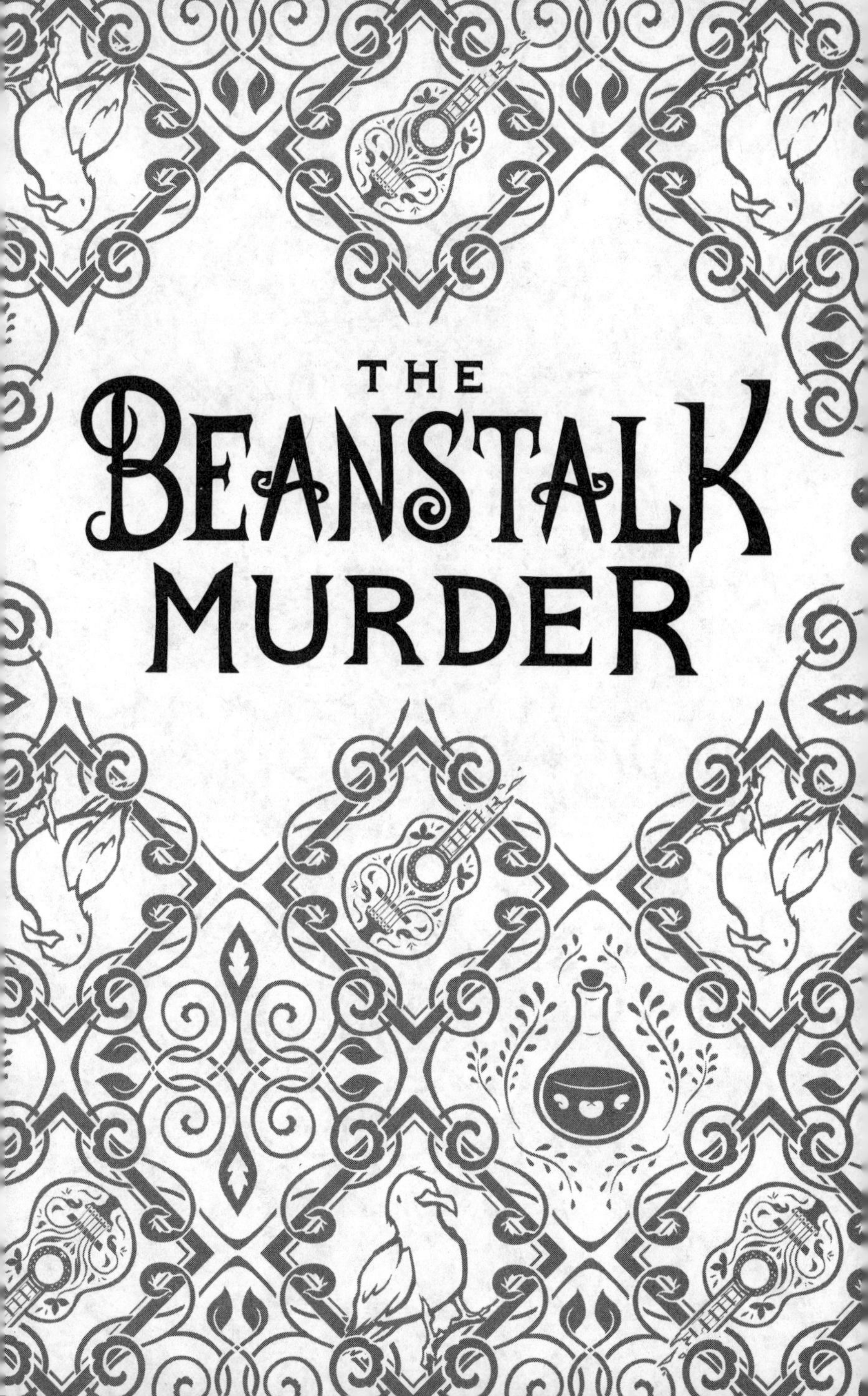
THE
BEANSTALK
MURDER

1

Mayhem at the Market

Anwen was hiding behind a horse.

She was doing her best to pretend that she wasn't hiding, of course—that she was, in fact, just standing there, minding her own business in a sheltered corner of the tavern stable yard—but she wasn't a very accomplished liar, even when she was lying to herself. She was hiding all right, and the thought of it was downright embarrassing. Not so embarrassing that she was about to stop doing it, though—Cerys Powell was out there somewhere, and Anwen really didn't want to bump into her.

As hiding places went, this was quite a good one. By peering around the horse's backside, she could see most of the busy market crowd without being seen herself. She stroked the horse's flank as her eyes darted from person to person, searching for the telltale flashes of golden hair or sea-blue dress that meant Cerys was on the prowl.

"I don't see her anywhere," she told the horse. "Perhaps she already left for the Academy."

The beast snorted and flicked its tail in her face.

“There’s no need to be like that,” Anwen said. “I know you’re hungry, but I already told you I haven’t got any food. And don’t pretend you didn’t understand me, because I’m fluent in horse, I’ll have you know. Well, fluent in pony, actually, but it’s virtually the same thing.”

She realized this last statement had been a mistake when the horse huffed and stamped its hoof, narrowly missing her toes. Anwen sighed.

“Fine, I know when I’ve worn out my welcome,” she said. “Honestly, why do horses have to be so snobbish?”

Cautiously, she stepped out from behind the animal. She felt exposed, and her hand went instinctively to the sprig of lucky heather woven through the untidy thatch of her hair. *Come on, Anwen*, she thought. *You’ve got a job to do.* Feeling a little more confident, she smoothed down her green woolen dress and made her way into the market square.

The village of Old Stump wasn’t a big place—just a handful of cottages, the tavern, and a mill, all built from rough gray slate and topped with roofs of shaggy green turf, studded with the last of the summer’s wildflowers. They all stood, as the village’s name implied, on the stump of one of the huge magic beanstalks that had dotted the landscape in the days when giants still roamed freely. As a result, Old Stump sat a few yards above the surrounding countryside, and Anwen could see all the way to the shimmering line of the sea on the eastern horizon, and to the shadows of the Usbrid Woods in the west.

Farmers and traders from every point in between had gathered for the village's weekly market. Anwen relaxed a little as she made her way through the crowd, taking in everything that the stalls had to offer. There was Farmer Pendaran with his wool and mutton; Farmer Pebin with his apples; Meredith, the tall, elderly fisherwoman, who had rowed upriver from the coast with her barrels of salted fish and live crabs.

Anwen watched Meredith swat away a cloud of pixies that were hovering around her stall. They were knobbly little creatures, bald and ugly, but with beautiful butterfly wings that shimmered like stained glass as they darted out of Meredith's reach, jeering and pulling faces at her.

"Filthy creatures!" Meredith snapped. She tucked a lock of her sleek gray hair behind one ear and sighed. "Anwen, do you know where that good-for-nothing minstrel's got to? It's his job to keep these things under control."

"You mean Stillpike?" asked Anwen. "Sorry, I haven't seen him."

Meredith made a grab for a particularly brazen pixie, and missed. "You're good with animals," she said. "Can't you persuade them to go and pester someone else?"

"Magical creatures are different," Anwen replied. "Pixies won't listen to me. Unless . . ."

"Unless what?"

A smile spread across Anwen's face as an idea took hold. "What if I transformed them into something that *would* listen to me?"

"You mean transfiguration?" Meredith suddenly looked doubtful. "That's High Magic. Can't you whip up something simple, like a charm or a warding spell? You know, some good old-fashioned Folk Magic."

"What if I transform them into butterflies?" said Anwen.

Meredith squinted down her nose. "Can you do that?"

"Of course," said Anwen. "I mean, they've already got the wings."

Meredith looked from Anwen to the pixies, who were now waggling their knobbly bottoms at her. "Fine," she sighed. "As long as you know what you're doing."

Anwen beamed. "Of course I do."

She didn't quite have the heart to tell Meredith

the truth—that transfiguration was indeed a delicate sort of High Magic, and she had only ever managed it once before, when she had turned an old shoelace into a worm. She'd been *trying* to turn it into a snake, but that was beside the point, and she was confident she could pull it off properly this time. She just needed to concentrate . . .

Closing her eyes, she raised her hands toward the pixies and tried to sense their presence with her mind. Then she began whispering the secret words of the spell, stumbling over the pronunciation of the ancient language as she focused on shifting the transformation from her imagination into reality. "Glöyn Byw, Glöyn Byw, rwy'n dy weld di, dere ataf i."

She felt a little spark of power slip out of her into the world, heard the *snap!* of the spell taking effect, and opened her eyes to admire her handiwork.

The pixies had certainly changed. But instead of butterflies, they were now a swarm of large, angry hornets.

Anwen's heart sank. "Bother," she said. "I was sure I'd got it right."

"Change them back!" Meredith cried, throwing her arms up to shield herself as the swarm surrounded her. "Quickly!"

"I haven't learned the counterspell yet," said Anwen, trying in vain to shoo the insects away from Meredith. "But if we wait a bit, they should change back automatically."

"Should?" said Meredith. "How long?"

A hot prickle of embarrassment crept into Anwen's face. She was about to admit that she hadn't actually read that passage of the textbook when, with a series of fat, wet popping sounds, the pixies reverted to their natural form. "About that long," she said, breathing a sigh of relief.

"Get out of it! Go on!" Meredith batted a few of the creatures away. The others darted back out of reach and resumed their taunting.

"I told you I only needed a simple spell," said Meredith. "Of course, if Stillpike could be bothered to show up and do his job, I wouldn't need one at all."

"Slander!" said a voice behind Anwen. "Some people have no respect for our hardworking veterans."

Anwen turned and found herself face-to-face with a small man in a military greatcoat. His thinning hair was slicked back, his face was lined and shrewd, and he wore a pencil mustache that looked as if it had been painted on with ink. He greeted them both with a wink that immediately lifted Anwen's mood.

"Ladies. Colonel Auric Stillpike, war hero and teller of mighty tales, at your service."

More like tall tales, thought Anwen. Everyone for miles around knew that Stillpike had bought his military coat from a wandering salesman, and that most of the medals pinned to his chest were from agricultural shows, including one for Most Amusingly Shaped Rhubarb.

"It's about time," said Meredith. "I pay you to keep these little pests away from my stock." She swatted at the pixies again.

"So do a lot of other discerning stallholders," Stillpike replied. "And some of them are willing to pay extra for more prompt attention. Perhaps I could interest you in my premium service?"

Meredith gave him a hard stare. "Just get rid of them."

Stillpike turned to Anwen with a look of exaggerated anguish. "D'you see how she treats me, m'dear? The man who fought off a battalion of giants, single-handed, in the Great Beanstalk War?"

Anwen laughed. "The Great Beanstalk War ended almost a century ago. You're not that old."

His expression brightened in an instant. "I'm delighted you think so. Fresh air and clean living, that's the secret to my youthful good looks." He waggled his eyebrows conspiratorially and swung back to Meredith. "And now, my good lady, let's deal with these pesky pixies."

"Finally," said Meredith.

Stillpike pulled a miniature guitar from the folds of his coat. The instrument was old and battered, but, when he struck a chord, it rang out clearly. It was a happy sound that lifted Anwen's spirits still further, but that was nothing compared to the pixies' reaction—they stopped flitting about and turned as one toward the sound, their eyes wide.

"Come along, my pretties," said Stillpike, strumming the chord again, then adding a second and third. "Follow the Colonel, and he'll play to your hearts' content." He repeated the three chords, layering in some plucked strings until the music became a happy little jig. He danced backward and the pixies followed, mesmerized. "See? No magic required, just natural talent." He grinned as he skipped away into the crowd, the pixies trailing after him. "Always a pleasure, ladies."

"The cheek of that man," said Meredith, watching him go.

"I quite like him," said Anwen.

"There's no accounting for taste. But enough about him. I take it you're here with my order?"

Anwen straightened, suddenly remembering that

she was supposed to be on business. "Oh, that's right." She pulled a small glass bottle, filled with what looked like olive oil, from her dress pocket and held it out. "Grandma mixed it for you this morning. Oil of Good Fortune. Just sprinkle it over your fishing nets, and they'll always catch something. Guaranteed effective from one full moon to the next."

"This is the sort of magic I'm talking about," said Meredith, accepting the bottle. "No fancy incantations, just simple, everyday spellcraft. What does your grandma want in return?"

"Four salted herring, please."

Meredith pocketed the bottle, pulled the fish from one of the barrels, wrapped them in cloth, and handed them over. "Give your grandma my regards," she said. "From one old boot to another."

Anwen grinned. "I will."

She started back through the market, and her thoughts returned to the failed transfiguration spell. Months of study, poring over her textbook late at night when her other duties were all finished, and she still didn't seem any closer to mastering it. What did she keep doing wrong?

"There you are, ditch witch."

Anwen froze. Then, with a sinking feeling in her stomach, she turned around.

Three girls stood before her—one tall and square, one small and mouselike, both wearing rough woolen dresses similar to her own. But the girl in the middle was different. Her golden hair cascaded over the folds of a beautiful sea-blue dress, which glimmered like sunlight on water. It even behaved like water—the fabric flowed and broke into tiny white-capped waves that gathered like lace at the hem. It was the best glamour magic Anwen had ever seen, and she burned with envy at the sight of it. Cerys always found a way to make her feel shabby and awkward, without even trying. She would sooner die than let Cerys know this, of course, so she puffed out her chest and set her face in what she hoped was a dignified expression.

"There's no such thing as a ditch witch, Cerys Powell," Anwen said haughtily. "I'm a Meadow Witch, as you very well know."

"You're only an apprentice," said Cerys. "And you don't live in a meadow, you live in a ditch."

"I live on the bank of a stream," Anwen replied.

Cerys tilted her heart-shaped face to one side and flashed a smile without a hint of warmth in it. "I don't care," she said. "I know what you're doing, and you're going to stop it."

"I haven't done anything." But that was a lie, and

she could already feel a guilty blush starting behind her ears.

"Don't deny it," said Cerys. "You're sending the seagull."

Anwen fought to stop the blush spreading to her face. "What seagull?"

"The one that's been following me all week," said Cerys. "The one that waits outside my house each morning. The one that . . ." She trailed off, apparently unable to get the words out.

"The one that what?" asked Anwen, biting the insides of her cheeks.

"The one that keeps pooing on me!" Cerys snapped.

It was finally too much, and Anwen let out a great snort of laughter.

"It's not funny," Cerys retorted, while her friends both glowered disapprovingly. "Every time I step outside it starts dive-bombing me. And I know you told it to!"

Anwen took a moment to restore her composure and, choosing not to risk another lie, looked up into the clear blue sky. "I can't see a seagull anywhere," she said.

"Because Bronwen and Efa keep chasing it off," said Cerys, nodding to her friends. "I can't spend all day sheltering indoors if I'm leaving for the Academy of High Magic tomorrow. I've got to buy things for the journey." She put her nose in the air and looked down it at Anwen. "Tell your bird to leave me alone, ditch witch. I don't want it following me all the way to the capital."

Anwen, who had been preparing to issue a reluctant confession, felt her anger flare. "Stop calling me a ditch witch," she growled. "Just because you're going to the Academy doesn't mean you're better than me."

"That's exactly what it means," said Cerys. She flicked the heather in Anwen's hair, dislodging a few petals. Anwen clamped a hand over them. "Lucky flowers and chatting to animals might be all right for you Folk Magic types," Cerys continued, "but the Academy wants genuine talent, which is why I'm going to become a fully qualified glamourist, and you're staying here. In your ditch."

Anwen stamped her foot. "The only reason I didn't pass my entrance exam is because you sabotaged it!"

"Me?" said Cerys. "I wasn't even in the room. You messed it up because you can't handle High Magic, and now you're taking it out on me with that stupid seagull."

Anwen could feel her face burning, but she no longer cared. "I should send a whole flock of them after you," she said. "It would serve you right. And just wait, I'll apply to the Academy again next year, and I'll get in."

"Try it," said Cerys. "After the disaster you caused, I doubt they'll even bother opening your application. How long did they say it would take for the examiner's eyebrows to grow back?"

Bronwen and Efa snickered, and Anwen balled her fists as her anger reached boiling point. She didn't care how much trouble it got her into, she wanted to knock Cerys flat on her back.

But before she could move, there was a guttural shriek high above them. All four girls looked up, and Anwen saw the silhouette of a bird flash across the sun. Something fell from it with a wet SPLAT! and Cerys cried out in dismay. Slowly, with a mix of triumph and trepidation, Anwen lowered her gaze.

Cerys stood rigid as a statue as a thick yellow trail of bird droppings oozed down her face and dripped onto the shifting surface of her dress. Bronwen and Efa gasped in horror. Passersby stopped and stared.

"This is your fault," Cerys hissed.

Anwen swallowed, uncomfortably aware of all the attention they were now attracting. "If it makes you feel any better, getting hit with bird poo is supposed to be lucky," she said.

Cerys answered with an incoherent howl of fury. Her concentration broken, the glamour spell surrounding her dress stuttered and died, revealing plain gray fabric, heavily patched and mended, underneath. "You think you're so clever, Anwen Sedge," she shrieked as Efa and Bronwen produced handkerchiefs and hastily wiped at the mess on her face. "You're nothing but a useless ditch witch. And that's all you'll ever be!"

More people were stopping to gawp now, and Anwen's face felt so hot she was surprised it hadn't spontaneously combusted. "Oh yes?" she said, with as much dignity as she could muster. "Well, I'm going back to my ditch to practice High Magic until I'm better at it than you." Then she turned and marched away, her heart thumping.

She didn't look back until she reached the slope leading out of the village, where she flopped against the wall of the tavern and deflated like an old balloon. She was still angry, both at Cerys, for the things she had said, and at herself for being found out so easily—if only she'd called off the seagull a few days ago, Cerys would never have suspected a thing. Now half the market knew what had happened, which meant that word was bound to get back to Anwen's grandmother. And she was not going to be happy.

"Well done, Anwen," she muttered to herself. "Another stupid mistake."

She was so stressed that her head was filling with a high-pitched whistling noise. She screwed her eyes shut and rubbed at her temples, but the noise only got louder. Louder and deeper.

She opened her eyes, and realized that the sound wasn't in her head at all. The bustle in the square died away as shoppers and stallholders looked around in confusion, trying to pinpoint the source of the sound. It seemed to be coming from everywhere.

Then a shadow appeared on the ground, growing larger by the second until it engulfed the whole square. Anwen raised her face to the sky, and gasped.

Something was up there. Something big enough to blot out the sun, and it was getting closer, fast. The whistle was the sound it made as it plunged through the air, and Anwen just had time to realize that the thing looked like a person before the market descended into total panic. People screamed and ran, abandoning their stalls and baskets in the rush to get clear. It was a stampede, and it swept Anwen with it, carrying her out of the village in the seconds before the enormous thing crashed down on the square with a noise like a mountain splitting in two.

The ground leapt, tossing people into the air like

toys. Anwen spun end over end, terrified and helpless, before cold water closed around her. She swallowed a mouthful and resurfaced, spluttering.

She had landed in the stream that skirted the village. Its waters slopped and rolled, breaking over the banks and sending flocks of nesting birds screaming into the sky. The dull roar of the gigantic thing's impact went with them, spreading out across the fields in an almighty echo.

Anwen hauled herself onto the bank and collapsed, trembling with shock. People lay scattered around her, some of them unconscious, others stunned and moaning. She forced herself to her feet, staggered onto the road leading into the village, and gave a small cry of disbelief.

Old Stump was gone, flattened beneath the bulk of the fallen thing, which now loomed in front of her like a low hill. As the dust settled, Anwen was able to make out more details. It was shrouded in enormous folds of material: She saw gold embroidery and sprays of white lace as big as ships' sails. Stranger still, two things like monoliths now stood on either side of the slope leading into the square. They were wide with a flat surface, and stood almost three times her height, tapering toward the sky. It took her a moment to realize they were the soles of an enormous pair of feet, shod in some kind of silk slippers, their toes pointing at the sun.

That was when she finally understood what she was looking at and had to sit down before the shock of it knocked her over.

This was a giant.

2
A Giant Crime Scene

Anwen was still sitting in the road, staring at the fallen giant, when she heard the familiar creak of a door nearby.

"What on earth . . . ?" a voice exclaimed.

She turned toward the stream beside the road. A mighty oak tree overhung the opposite bank, its knotted roots stretching down to the water's edge. They formed a circular hollow in the slope, into which a bright red wooden door had been set. This was the home she shared with her grandmother. A hand-painted sign nailed to the trunk read,

EIRA SEDGE (& APPRENTICE)—MEADOW WITCH
FOLK MAGIC SERVICES AND CONSULTATIONS
(HOUSEHOLD CHARMS, MIDWIFERY,
HEALING POTIONS, BURIAL RITES, ETC.)

The door stood open, and Eira's moonlike face poked out.

"Well, that's just made my afternoon more complicated." She scurried out the door, across a stepping-stone in the middle of the stream, and up onto the road, wheezing slightly.

Eira Sedge was small and round, and looked as if she'd been partially knitted. Despite the summer sun, she wore a heavy woolen shawl over her dress and fingerless gloves on her hands. Her gray hair was piled up in an untidy bun, pinned in place with a pair of knitting needles.

She surveyed the scattering of shell-shocked villagers, then hurried to Anwen's side, pulled her to her feet, and patted her down.

"It's a giant, Grandma," said Anwen, slightly dazed.

"Yes, I can see that," Eira replied.

"Then shouldn't we get out of here?" said Anwen. "Before he gets up?"

"I don't think he's in any hurry," said Eira, clasping Anwen's head in both hands and peering closely at her pupils. "He's dead."

The word rang in Anwen's head like a bell. "Dead . . ."

"As a doornail," said Eira. "The poor soul fell out of the Sky Kingdom into our world. That's a very long drop, even for a giant."

"But . . . but that's terrible!"

"Yes, it is, but right now I'm more worried about you." Eira released Anwen's head and took hold of her arms instead, bending them this way and that. "I can't find any injuries. Are you hurt?"

"I . . . I don't think so."

The examination stopped abruptly. "Then why didn't you say so? Don't just stand there, help me with the wounded."

It was almost a relief to be told what to do, and Anwen's confidence returned as she followed her grandmother from person to person, checking for broken bones and concussions, and helping to treat cuts and bruises. Those who were well enough were enlisted to join the aid effort, and within fifteen minutes the two witches had established a makeshift field hospital in the road between the giant's feet. It wasn't much—just a wonky table and a handful of chairs salvaged from the rubble of the tavern—but it was enough to draw people together, whether injured or not, and a nervous crowd soon gathered in front of it.

Anwen spotted Cerys among them, still accompanied by Bronwen and Efa. She looked shocked and dusty, but had taken the time to restore the glamour magic around her dress, and even added a collar of white-capped waves when she caught Anwen looking.

Fine, don't help, Anwen thought, and turned back to her work. There was certainly plenty to keep her busy, and she spent the next hour shuttling back and forth to the oak tree, fetching healing herbs and potions for Eira, who diagnosed each patient with an expert eye.

Remarkably, everyone who had been at the market was soon accounted for and, with the exception of a few broken bones and concussions, there were no serious injuries.

"This calls for a ballad!" announced Stillpike, who had been leading the pixies out into the fields at the time of the disaster. He struck up a rousing song on his guitar, and people clapped and sang along, albeit somewhat groggily.

"It could have been worse," said Meredith, who had arrived at the field hospital nursing a sprained wrist. "I sprinkled myself with your Oil of Good Fortune as I ran, Eira, and when the giant landed, I got thrown into a hay bale. A nice soft landing. Ouch!" She flinched as Anwen tightened a bandage around her wrist.

"Sorry," said Anwen. "But if you landed in the hay bale, how did you hurt yourself?"

Meredith looked embarrassed. "I tripped on my way here," she said. "I was coming to help."

"Silly old goose," said Eira, who was furiously mashing ingredients in a large stone bowl. "A woman of your age should watch where she's going."

"I'm the same age as you, you old battle-ax," Meredith replied. "Maybe you should make your luck potions a bit stronger."

"Nobody warned me it was going to start raining giants," said Eira.

The two women glared at each other, then burst out laughing, but Anwen slapped a hand to her forehead in sudden frustration.

"Oh no!" she said. "The salted herring you gave me! I must have dropped them when I landed in the stream."

Eira wiped a tear from her eye. "We'll survive, my dear. Besides, we've got bigger problems to deal with." She tipped the contents of the mixing bowl into a small cauldron that was bubbling on a camping stove. "This white birch tea is almost ready," she said. "It's a natural painkiller, and I've stirred in some dewdrops gathered on the solstice for a bit of extra magical kick. Help yourself to a cup, Meredith, and dish it out to anyone else who needs some."

"Gladly," Meredith replied. "But why can't you do it?"

"Because Anwen and I have another job to do."

"What's that?" asked Anwen.

Her grandmother dusted off her hands. "We're going to examine this giant."

The giant was big. His feet straddled the western entrance to the village square, while his head blocked the road leading out of it to the east, forcing Anwen and Eira to make their way through the surrounding fields to get from one end of the body to the other.

The closer they got to the giant's head, the more apprehensive Anwen became. She'd seen dead bodies before, of course—one of the most important services a Meadow Witch could offer was preparing the dead for burial—but she'd never seen a giant up close. No living person had. She'd heard plenty of horror stories, though—of their bloated faces and jaundiced, warty skin. Of their baleful eyes that seemed to stare right through you. But most of all, she'd heard about their gaping maws full of crooked tombstone teeth, perfect for grinding human beings into jelly.

So it was a bit of an anticlimax to discover, when they rounded the giant's shoulder, that he actually looked quite normal. His face was narrow, his skin smooth, and his lips slightly parted, revealing a neat row of teeth that shone like pearls. Black, lustrous hair lay in an untidy fan around his head. If it wasn't for his deathly pallor, he could have been asleep.

"Oh," said Anwen. "He doesn't look very monstrous."

"You shouldn't put too much faith in Stillpike's old war stories," said Eira. "As far as I know, giants are people, the same as you and me. They're just bigger."

"That's an understatement," said Anwen. "He's the size of the whole village."

"A hundred and ten . . . maybe a hundred and twenty feet from head to toe, would be my guess," said Eira. "Which reminds me, you'll need this." She pulled a small leather-bound book and a stick of charcoal from her apron pocket. "We need to write down our observations."

Anwen groaned. "You mean *I* need to write down our observations. You're turning this into a lesson, aren't you?"

"You're my apprentice," Eira replied. "Everything's a lesson."

With a great show of reluctance, Anwen took the book and opened it. It was filled with untidy notes from previous lessons, interspersed with sketches of flowers, people, and animals that she had done while bored.

"Take a good look at our giant," said Eira. "What's the most interesting thing you notice?"

"He's huge?"

"I said the most interesting thing, not the most obvious. Try again."

What could be more interesting than that? Anwen thought, but held her tongue and looked more closely. "His clothes?" she asked. "They're really fancy."

Eira nodded. "Certainly the finest I've seen in a

good many years," she said. "Not even the local magistrate dresses this well."

Anwen gave a satisfied grin. It was so obvious now that she'd seen it. The giant wore a long golden frock coat with matching waistcoat and breeches, a ruffled shirt of lavender silk, and a shining white cravat. Just visible at the opposite end of Old Stump were the tips of his white silk slippers, embroidered with gold thread.

"So he's rich," she said.

"Most giants are," said Eira. "Their whole society revolves around gold, you see. That's one of the reasons the Great Beanstalk War started—after centuries of living together peacefully, people down here saw all the gold up there and got greedy."

Anwen pictured gold coins the size of cart wheels, piled as high as mountains. "How did we fight against people this big?" she asked.

"With magic," said Eira. "For all their size, giants can't use magic at all. It's why the war ended in a stalemate."

A world without magic, thought Anwen. *What a strange place the Sky Kingdom must be*. "I wonder who he was," she said.

"That's one of the questions we've got to answer," said Eira. "And as quickly as possible."

"What's the rush?"

"There hasn't been any contact between the human world and the giants since the war ended," said Eira. "Both sides signed a treaty—the giants stay in their world and we stay in ours. No exceptions."

"So how did he get here?" asked Anwen.

"He must have fallen through one of the thin places," said Eira. She peered straight up into the sky, shielding her eyes from the sun.

"Thin places?" Anwen turned to a fresh page in her book and scribbled the words down.

"Holes in the world," said Eira. "Gaps that lead from one realm to another." She lowered her gaze, held her hands out in front of her, palms downward, and placed one on top of the other. "Our worlds are layered, like this," she said. "Humans underneath, giants up above. The thin places are like doorways between the two layers."

"So the thin places are all up there?" Anwen pointed upward.

"Exactly. That's why most people call the giants' realm the Sky Kingdom. They don't actually live in the sky, of course, it's just the only way to reach it."

"And that's what the magic beanstalks were for."

Eira nodded. "Old Stump used to be the site of a beanstalk, so it stands to reason there's a thin place above it."

Anwen squinted at the sky, half hoping to see a collection of giants staring back at her, but it was blue and empty. "Are the holes invisible?"

"Until you stumble into them," said Eira. "Which is what I *had* assumed happened to this poor fellow."

Something about her grandmother's tone made Anwen turn to her. "But?"

"But," said Eira, "that was before I got a good look at him. And there's something wrong."

"Apart from him being dead, you mean?"

"It's a question of *how* dead," said Eira. "I've worked with cadavers all my life, and this man does not look like he passed away within the last hour."

Anwen looked at the giant again. Yes, his skin was smooth, but it was also slightly waxy, and she knew that dead bodies got like that after a day or so, if you didn't keep them cold. "Maybe giants' bodies work differently?"

"Maybe," said Eira. "But I want you to make a careful note of everything we see here. Sooner or later, someone official is going to start asking questions, and I want to make sure we have some answers for them."

Anwen nodded, suddenly businesslike. She scribbled down a summary of all the things they had discussed, then turned a page, sat down in the grass, and made a sketch of the giant's profile. It seemed like a sensible idea to keep a record of his features—people asked her to do that at funerals sometimes, as a keepsake of the face they would never see again.

When her sketch was complete, she got up and dusted the grass from her bottom. "I'm going to go around and draw him from the other side too," she told Eira, who was inspecting the stitching of the giant's collar. "In case he's got any distinguishing features or anything."

"Good idea," Eira said. "Come back and find me when you're finished."

Anwen kicked through the long grass and poppies as she made her way around the top of the giant's head. It took her a couple of minutes, as she had to cross the road heading east out of the village, and negotiate a turnip field on the other side.

Will anyone up there in the Sky Kingdom miss this face? she wondered, reviewing her sketch as she walked. Drawing someone always made her feel closer to them, and she realized that her view of the giant had shifted in the last few minutes. He was no longer just a thing that had crashed down into her life, but a person. A problem, yes, and a total stranger. But a person, at least.

"I hope I don't have to bury you, though," she said to the fallen body. "That would be a lot of work."

She reached the middle of the field and sat down with her back to the stream, ready to start her new sketch. That was when she looked up at the giant's face and saw the wound.

It was small but serious—an ugly bruise just above his eye, speckled with a few drops of dried blood. Anwen sketched it quickly, her sense of disquiet growing with every stroke of the charcoal. Something about that wound was wrong.

By the time she snapped her notebook shut, she knew what it was.

"It's on the front of his head," she told Eira as they stood together examining the wound fifteen minutes later. "But he landed on his back, so it can't be an injury caused by the fall. It must have happened in the Sky Kingdom, before he fell through the thin place."

Eira nodded. "I've always said you've got a good eye for detail, if you'll only learn a little patience. What else can you tell me?"

"He hasn't sustained any other injuries," said Anwen. "I asked a family of field mice to check his scalp over, in case there was another wound hidden by his hair, but they didn't find anything."

"Good thinking," said Eira. "Anything else?"

“His injury isn’t fresh. I can’t be sure, but it looks a few hours old.”

Eira’s expression was grim. “At least twelve. Which confirms my worst suspicion.”

“What’s that?”

“That this giant’s death was no accident, and he didn’t fall into our world by mistake. The blow to the head killed him sometime last night, and then his body was dumped here.”

“You mean . . .” Anwen left the question unspoken.

“Yes,” said Eira. “This was murder.”

3

The Seed of a Plan

Murder! Eira's verdict sent a chill through Anwen, and she took an unconscious step away from the fallen giant's body. Murders were only supposed to happen in distant cities, or in scary fireside tales. They weren't supposed to happen in Old Stump.

"What should we do?" she asked.

Eira scratched her chin thoughtfully. "A Meadow Witch works with nature for the good of those around her," she said. "This giant died *un*naturally, which means the world is out of balance until we set it right."

"We can't exactly bring him back to life."

"No," said Eira. "But we can do our best to bring him justice."

"How?" asked Anwen. "Whoever killed him is in the Sky Kingdom. We can't get anywhere near it."

Eira peered into the sky. "There might be a way," she said slowly. "I'll need some High Magic, though."

Anwen's eyes widened in excitement. "Let me help! I've been practicing."

Eira pursed her lips. "We agreed you were going to drop this idea of leaving for the Academy."

"It wouldn't be until next year," Anwen replied.

"And your apprenticeship runs for another two. I won't let you throw away your future as a Meadow Witch to go chasing dreams of glory in the big city."

Anwen shifted uncomfortably. "Maybe I want to be more than just a Meadow Witch."

"Just?" said Eira, lifting an eyebrow. "Am I *just* a Meadow Witch?"

Anwen looked at her feet. "That's not what I meant. And I really could help."

Eira folded her arms. "You can help by fetching Cerys Powell."

The words struck Anwen like a slap of cold water. "What? Why her?"

But Eira had already set off toward the giant's feet. "Because she's the only person for miles who can work glamour magic," she called over her shoulder. "And while you're at it, you can apologize to her about that incident with the seagull. Don't think I hadn't heard. I expect better from you."

Anwen followed, resentment hanging over her like a cloud. Why did Cerys stupid Powell always get the best of everything?

Anwen's mood had not improved by the time she and Eira reached the field hospital, where Meredith was still doling out cups of tea. Anwen glowered at the crowd until she spotted Cerys, nursing a steaming cup alongside Efa and Bronwen. Cerys's parents had joined them, fussing and fretting over her like a pair of nesting birds. Anwen's heart sank through her stomach—she was going to have to apologize in front of all of them.

"Bring Cerys over here, please," said Eira. "And once the two of you have made up, I want you to take a page from your notebook and write a message to the giants. Tell them what's happened, but keep it short and simple. And as neat as you can, please."

"For the giants?" said Anwen. "Are you sure?"

"Positive," Eira replied. "I'll be right back. I just need to find something I once put away for safekeeping."

She hurried off in the direction of the cottage, leaving Anwen to drag herself over to Cerys and the others.

"Hello," Anwen mumbled.

Cerys's nose wrinkled in displeasure. "What do you want?"

Anwen really had been preparing to apologize, but Cerys's tone made the words stick in her throat. "My grandma wants you," she said at last.

"What for?" said Cerys.

Anwen shrugged. "It's something to do with the giant."

"Isn't it terrible?" said Cerys's father. He was a tall, ruddy-faced man, with a thick ginger beard that only half hid his look of shock. "We were feeding the pigs in the yard when it happened. The whole farm shook, didn't it, Rhi?" He nudged his wife, who was busy combing dried bird droppings out of Cerys's hair. "We got here as quick as we could. To think, our poor Cerys was almost squashed."

"Along with the rest of us," said Anwen, but he gave no indication that he had heard her.

"I'm worried about the mail coach," said Cerys's mother, who boasted the same blond curls and heart-shaped face as her daughter. "It won't be able to get through tomorrow if that brute's still blocking the road."

"Are you expecting a letter?" said Anwen, confused by the sudden shift in the conversation.

"The coach is going to take me to the Academy, of course," Cerys replied. "Daddy's booked me a seat."

"And not on the roof," her father said. "Inside!" He put his arm around Cerys and beamed. "Nothing but the best for my special girl."

Cerys hugged him back, and sneered at Anwen, who decided to end the conversation before she said something she might regret.

"I'll be at the table when you're ready," she said, and plodded away.

She dropped into one of the battered chairs between the giant's feet, shoved Eira's mixing bowl aside, and opened her notebook to a blank page. Cerys drifted over with her parents as she began writing:

Murdered giant dumped on human world.
Identity unknown.

"Murdered?" said Cerys, reading over her shoulder.

The word was taken up by others nearby, and passed among the crowd until it was on every pair of lips.

Meredith arrived at a run, ladle still in hand. "What's all this about a murder?" she asked.

Anwen's reply was interrupted by sudden sounds of destruction from her and Eira's cottage across the stream—crashes, bangs, and the splintering of wood. It sounded as if floorboards were being ripped up.

"Someone in the Sky Kingdom killed the giant and dropped his body on Old Stump," Anwen replied.

"Skulduggery!" said Stillpike, appearing at Meredith's side. "Trust those giants to be up to no good. We should retaliate."

"Don't be ridiculous," said Meredith.

"Those monsters don't frighten me," said Stillpike.

"Only because you've never seen a live one," said Meredith.

Stillpike's mouth dropped open. "Madam, are you calling my proud history of military service into question?" He winked at Meredith, who huffed impatiently and cast a wary glance in the direction of Eira's cottage. The noises had stopped.

"I hope your grandma's got a better plan," she said.

"I don't know," Anwen replied. "She just asked me to write this message for the giants."

"That's stupid," said Cerys. "How are they ever going to see it?"

"With the help of your magic, young lady!" came Eira's voice. She stepped into the circle, covered in dust and cobwebs but looking very pleased with herself. She carried a small chest, hardly eight inches in length, made of pitted green metal. "Good work," she said, peering over Anwen's shoulder at the notebook. "But you'd better add a line asking them to come and collect the body."

Stillpike started in alarm. "You're inviting the giants down here?"

"Certainly," said Eira. "We can't leave an enormous corpse on top of the village, and we can't possibly move it by ourselves. The giants will have to do it for us."

"Won't that be dangerous?" asked Meredith.

"Possibly," Eira replied. "But I can't see any alternative. If we don't contact the giants, whoever killed this poor soul might strike again. What if they dump another body on us? I don't want to spend the rest of my days watching the skies, waiting for something terrible to happen, do you?"

The question sent a wave of subdued chatter through the crowd.

"How is my magic supposed to help?" said Cerys.

"Good question," said Anwen, looking pointedly at her grandmother.

"You know glamour magic, Cerys," said Eira. "You can make people see whatever you want them to."

Cerys obviously took this as a compliment, as her hair suddenly acquired a tiara of curling turquoise waves to match her dress. "And I'm entirely self-taught."

"Then I'm sure you can make this page of Anwen's notebook look a hundred times bigger than it really is," Eira replied. She tore the page out of the book and handed it to Cerys.

"A hundred?" said Cerys. Her eyes darted nervously between the page and her dress.

She can't do both spells at once! Anwen thought gleefully. "Maybe you should ask Cerys for something easier, Grandma," she said, her words dripping with false sympathy.

Cerys didn't reply. She just drew her hand over the page, and Anwen was forced to jump back as something the size of a ship's sail suddenly unfurled in front of her. It was the page from her notebook, but impossibly large. Each of her handwritten letters was five feet tall. People gasped and applauded as its shadow fell over them.

Anwen turned a critical eye on Cerys and saw that her dress had faded to little more than a rough blue shape, fuzzy at the edges, and that her tiara had disappeared completely. Anwen reached out and prodded the enormous sheet with the tip of her finger. It passed straight through.

"It's just a projection, silly. Look." Cerys waved something in Anwen's face—it was the real notebook page, still its proper size. The projection waved at the same time, sweeping back and forth across the road, and causing several people in the crowd to turn and run.

"Splendid, Cerys," said Eira. "That's exactly what I wanted."

"It's nothing," Cerys replied with a flick of her hair. "At least," she added in a whisper just loud enough for Anwen to hear, "not for those of us with some actual skill."

Anwen clenched her jaw and seethed in silence.

"This is all very impressive, ladies," said Stillpike, "but as big as the message is, it's still not visible from the Sky Kingdom."

"I know," said Eira. "That's why we have to send it to them."

"How are we going to do that?" asked Anwen.

Eira looked solemn but couldn't keep the sparkle of excitement from her eyes. "With this," she said, patting the small chest. "My mother salvaged it during the war and made me promise never to use it except in an emergency. I think murder counts, don't you?" She opened the chest, and Anwen, Cerys, Stillpike, and Meredith all craned forward to see what lay inside.

It resembled a pebble—a small, gray, dusty-looking thing, sitting in the corner of the otherwise empty chest.

Anwen's anticipation dissolved into disappointment. "What is it?" she asked.

"I think I know," said Meredith in an awed voice. "Oh, Eira, tell me I'm wrong. I've heard rumors that you had one hidden somewhere, but I didn't want to believe it."

Carefully, almost reverentially, Eira held the object up between finger and thumb. "It's a magic bean," she said. "One of the last in the whole country."

The crowd of onlookers gasped as one.

"But they're illegal!" said Anwen.

"So they should be," said Eira. "They're very dangerous things in the wrong hands. Officially, planting this would be an act of war."

"So what are you going to do with it?" asked Stillpike.

"Plant it, of course," said Eira. "Growing a magic beanstalk is the only way to reach the Sky Kingdom. I'm just going to do it . . . diplomatically. If we attach our written message to the top, we can send that up instead of going ourselves. It'll be less threatening."

Stillpike gave a short, harsh laugh. "Why should the giants feel threatened? They're the ones dropping dead bodies on us. Surely that's already in breach of the peace treaty?"

People murmured in agreement.

"I hate to admit it, but he's got a point," said Meredith. "Perhaps we should send word to the capital instead. Let the government handle this."

Eira waved the idea away like a bad smell. "They're two days' ride away," she said. "And what do you suppose they'll do when they get here? Stand around arguing for a week before they finally admit that someone has to contact the giants. That means planting one of their own official beans, and they won't dare try that without bringing in the army.

Half the country will be on a war footing before they even put the thing in the ground. No, it's better for both sides if we deal with this ourselves, quickly and quietly."

Anwen was positively fizzing with excitement now. Just a few hours earlier, she hadn't been looking forward to anything more exciting than salted herring, and now here she was, ready to reach out to another world. "So we send the message up to the Sky Kingdom on the beanstalk," she said. "The giants come down and retrieve the body. But then what?"

"Then they leave, we chop down the beanstalk, and tomorrow we start rebuilding Old Stump," said Eira.

"And I still get to leave for the Academy on time," added Cerys. "I like this plan."

That was enough to make Anwen dislike it on principle, but she didn't want to say so in front of Eira. At least she would get to see some living giants before all this was over.

"Right," said Eira. "We have everything we need. Let's plant this bean."

Eira led everyone out into the meadow immediately south of the giant. They made a slow and unusual procession: Eira held the chest containing the bean in front of her like some sort of holy relic, while Anwen and Cerys followed behind with the torn page of the notebook. The gigantic projection spell floated above them like a sail, fluttering silently. Behind them came Cerys's parents, then Meredith and Stillpike, who was strumming an upbeat tune on his guitar. Finally, the rest of the crowd followed, fussing and chattering until Eira signaled a halt beside the giant's elbow, which jutted out of a ruined house into the meadow.

"This should do," she said, kicking a rough divot into the soil with the toe of her clog. She opened the chest and withdrew the bean.

"Are you sure it's going to grow?" asked Anwen. "It looks dead."

"It's very old," said Eira. "But the magic inside it should still be strong." She motioned for Anwen and Cerys to come closer. "We might not have long to attach Anwen's message to the top of the beanstalk once it sprouts, so I need you to be ready," she said. "Two pairs of hands will do the job more quickly than one, so, Anwen, I want you to hold the paper, and Cerys, you can pin it to the stalk with this." She produced a brass tack from the folds of her shawl. "I've put quite a tough little fastening spell on it, so it should hold firm. Are you both ready?"

Anwen locked eyes with Cerys. "Yes, Grandma."

"Of course," said Cerys.

"Good. I want everyone else to stand back, please."

The crowd shuffled backward a few steps, but didn't go far. Eira held the bean up for them all to see. "I won't pretend to know everything that could happen once I plant this," she said. "But with a little luck, Old Stump will be back to normal before winter." She looked around the circle of faces. "Any objections?"

People shuffled their feet in silence.

"Then let's do it." Eira dropped the bean into the hole and scraped the earth over it with her foot.

They didn't have to wait long. Within a few seconds, a green shoot sprang up, unfurling brilliant emerald leaves as it twisted and strained toward the sky.

"Aha!" exclaimed Eira. "Quickly, girls, get the message ready."

She hustled Anwen and Cerys to the expanding stalk, which was now as thick as a man's arm and almost as tall as Anwen. More leaves budded from its sides, unfurling with a series of soft popping noises. Anwen held the page out in both hands and pulled it taut.

"Now!" said Eira. Cerys drove the tack through the page, into the firm green flesh of the plant. Anwen let go and moved to step back, but found that she couldn't—the hem of her sleeve was pinned to the beanstalk along with the paper. She pulled against it with all her strength, but the tack refused to give.

"Help!" she cried as the beanstalk dragged her arm—and the rest of her—steadily skyward. Her feet had just left the ground when Eira and Cerys both grabbed her around the waist. Their weight slowed her ascent, but her arm burned with the strain. She felt like the rope in tug-of-war, and the beanstalk was winning.

"The tack!" Eira shouted. "You've got to break the fastening spell!"

Anwen desperately moved the tip of her index finger in a clockwise circle over the tack, trying to unwind the spell, but nothing happened. "It's not working!" she cried.

Before Eira could answer, her grip failed and she fell back with a thud. At the same instant, the beanstalk quivered, groaned, and surged upward with the speed of a rocket.

Anwen caught her breath as the air whistled past her, plucking the heather from her hair and making her eyes sting. Within seconds she was surrounded by sky—a sea of brilliant blue, fading to milky white in the distance. It was only when she looked down to see how high she was that she realized Cerys was still hanging on to her.

"Heeeeelp!" Cerys squealed, her face a mask of terror.

Anwen almost screamed with shock. "Hold on!" she shouted.

"What do you think I'm doing, you idiot?" Cerys yelled back. "Get us down from here!"

But it was already far too late for that. The world spun away beneath them, shrinking until it was just a smudge of greens and browns, so remote and indistinct that it didn't seem real anymore. The Usbrid Woods lay like a rumpled blanket on the carpet of fields in the west and, on the distant horizon beyond them, Anwen could just make out a dark, smoky stain that must have been the capital. The sight was terrifying and wonderful, all at once.

Then it was gone, and a shock of raw magic ran down Anwen's body, stinging like ice water. The sky vanished, and the world around them was suddenly dark. There was a terrible crunching sound of stone against stone, and the air filled with dust. There was a smell of gas, so strong that it made Anwen gag. Cerys shouted in fear. Then, with a final, deafening smash, they burst back into daylight.

It was not the same daylight they had left behind, however—the sun shone with a coppery tint that Anwen had never seen before.

With another groan, the beanstalk's growth spurt slowed to a crawl, and then stopped altogether. Anwen spat the dust from her mouth and looked around.

The beanstalk had emerged into the Sky Kingdom from a pile of rubble so enormous, it looked like a small hill. Chunks of white marble the size of the Old Stump tavern lay everywhere, and, half-hidden among them, Anwen saw a dented statue of a giant, fashioned from gold.

"Did . . . did we make it?" asked Cerys, her voice trembling.

"Yes," said Anwen. "But I think we broke some public art."

There were sounds of commotion and, as the dust began to settle, Anwen saw that they were hanging about three hundred feet above the center of a vast city square. Grand buildings reared up all around it, and below them, giants ran in all directions. Most of them were dressed in gold finery and, to Anwen's amazement, they all looked terrified.

"It's an invasion!" someone shouted. "Fetch the guards!"

"Look what they've done to the memorial!"

"They're coming for our gold!"

Anwen's skin prickled with nervous goose bumps. "I don't think we've made a good first impression," she said. "Wasn't our message clear enough?" She looked up and realized that Cerys's projection spell had vanished. "Cerys!" she said. "You need to get the spell working again. Quickly!"

But Cerys had gone as white as the shattered marble, and the last of the glamour spell surrounding her dress had disappeared as well. "Forget that," she said, on the verge of tears. "We need to get out of here!" She let go of Anwen's waist and dropped onto the nearest leaf.

"I'm still stuck to this thing," snapped Anwen. She circled her finger over the tack again, but it still failed to give. "Get me free and recast the projection spell, before someone decides to squash us!"

The thunderous tramp of boots made them both look around. One whole side of the square was taken up by a mountainous building of crimson marble that could only have been a palace. It stood behind a wrought iron fence, in which a pair of gates had just swung open, and a team of soldiers in gleaming red-and-gold armor was hurrying out of it toward the beanstalk. They had their swords drawn.

"Look, Captain!" one of them said, pointing up at Anwen and Cerys. "Vermin!"

"We're not vermin, we're people!" Anwen shouted down to them. But even as the words left her mouth, she knew her voice was too small to carry in this world.

The squad reached the pile of rubble, and the Captain stepped forward. He was a handsome but stern-looking young man, with dark brown skin and keen hazel eyes. "We need to stop any more of the little monsters getting through," he said. "Men? Take the head off this beanstalk and eradicate those pests."

"Yes, sir!" The soldiers scrambled up the rubble and hacked at the stalk with their swords. Anwen's stomach lurched with fear.

"Hurry up, Cerys!"

No reply came, and she realized that the leaf to which Cerys had been clinging was empty.

"Cerys?" She scanned the leaves below her, but Cerys was gone.

"You coward!" Anwen screamed. "Don't just leave me here!"

The beanstalk shivered under the rain of blows, and she wondered how this could be happening—trapped, alone, and about to die in an alien world. *And all because you couldn't break the spell on a stupid brass tack*, she reflected. *No wonder the Academy wouldn't take you.*

Feeling thoroughly ashamed of herself, Anwen screwed her eyes shut and waited for the end.

4

Small People with Big Problems

Because she had her eyes shut, Anwen heard, rather than saw, the ripple of shock that ran through the giant guards. The sharp whistle of their swords came to a sudden halt, and the beanstalk stopped shuddering under their blows.

"Captain! Look!" one of them exclaimed.

Anwen opened one eye and laughed in surprise. Her handwritten note—or rather, Cerys's projection—was flying overhead, big enough for the whole plaza to see it. And shimmying down the beanstalk from a leaf directly above, as nimbly as a farm cat, was Cerys herself.

"I thought you'd run away," said Anwen.

"If that's supposed to be a thank-you, don't bother," said Cerys, plopping down onto a leaf beside her. "Because I really am leaving, and you need to come with me."

"I can't! I'm still stuck." She circled her finger over the tack again. "See?"

Cerys rolled her eyes. "It's *counter*clockwise, stupid." She circled her own finger in the opposite direction, and the tack slipped free of the beanstalk. "Honestly, can't you even get Folk Magic right?"

Anwen scowled at her as she tacked the notepaper back into place. "I had a lot on my mind, all right?"

They started down the beanstalk again, toward the wreckage of the statue.

"HALT!"

Both girls froze as the Captain took a bounding step forward, his hand raised.

"What's all this about a murdered giant?" he said, pointing at the projection. "Is it true?"

Anwen and Cerys nodded vigorously. Just a few minutes ago, Anwen had been excited by the prospect of seeing a living giant, but now that she was face-to-face with one, it was terrifying. She couldn't escape the thought that he could squash either of them to paste with a single jab of his thumb if he wanted to.

But she saw genuine worry in his eyes now. He sheathed his sword and stepped up close to the beanstalk, until his face was only a few yards below them. "Why, you're only children," he said, his breath like a hot summer wind in their faces. He turned to his men. "Put away your swords."

"But, Captain," one of the men protested. "What if it's a trap?"

"Just do it." He turned back to Anwen and Cerys. "The murdered giant. Describe him for me."

Anwen and Cerys exchanged a nervous look. "He's about a hundred and twenty feet tall," Anwen said, speaking as loudly as she could. "With thick black hair, and he's wearing a lot of gold. His shirt . . ." She trailed off as the Captain shook his head.

"I can't hear you properly," he said. "Your voice is too small."

Anwen grunted in frustration. Then an idea hit her. "Cerys," she said. "Can you change the projection spell?" She pulled her notebook from her pocket and flipped through the pages until she found the illustration she wanted.

Cerys rolled her eyes, but put her hand flat on the page and whispered the incantation. The first projection spell winked out overhead, and the new one unfurled in front of them, making the Captain leap back in surprise. It was the charcoal sketch that Anwen had made of the dead giant's face.

There was a moment of stunned silence as the Captain and his men processed what they were seeing. Then their mouths dropped open, and, beyond them, Anwen heard the crowd of onlookers gasp.

"But that's . . . !" one of the soldiers started.

The Captain silenced him with a look. "We all know who it is," he said sharply.

"What do we do, sir?" asked one of the others.

The Captain stared at the picture, and Anwen could practically see the thoughts racing behind his eyes. He didn't seem excited by any of his options.

Cerys nudged her in the ribs. "Who is it?" she hissed.

"I don't know," Anwen replied. "But he must have been someone important. Look at them all."

Behind the guards, the people of the Sky Kingdom were drifting back, keeping a wary distance from the beanstalk but drawn by Anwen's illustration. Most of them looked shocked or disbelieving. A few had even burst into tears.

"We'll take them to the palace," the Captain said. "We've got to break the news to Her Highness."

His men shuffled uncomfortably. "Are you sure that's wise, sir?" one of them asked. "What if they use their magic on her? You know how sneaky humans are." He managed to make *humans* sound like such a dirty word that Anwen felt her cheeks prickle with anger.

"If they try anything, they'll be dinner for the palace cats," said the Captain, making Cerys gasp. "But I don't think that's why they're here." He held the flat of his palm out toward the beanstalk, close enough for both girls to step onto. "I'll trust you if you trust me. Sound fair?"

Summoning her courage, Anwen sprang from the

beanstalk onto the Captain's outstretched hand. The skin of his palm was soft and a little springy, and she could feel the heat radiating from it as she sat down cross-legged. She gestured to Cerys, who shook her head.

"I'm not going anywhere near their stupid palace, or their stupid cats," said Cerys. "I hate it here. It's dangerous, and it smells bad."

"No, it doesn't," said Anwen.

"Then what's that stink?" demanded Cerys.

Anwen sniffed the air, and retched as a stench of rotting vegetables rolled over her. She covered her nose, but there was no disguising where the smell was coming from: the beanstalk.

At that same instant, Cerys gave a cry of dismay. The leaf on which she sat was turning black and curling up at the edges. The leaves surrounding it were withering as well, and a dark stain quickly spread from them into the beanstalk's trunk.

"Quickly, Cerys!" shouted Anwen. "Jump!"

Fear froze Cerys to the spot, until the Captain reached out with his free hand and plucked her from the leaf a second before it crumbled into ash.

"That was close," he said as he placed her gently on his palm beside Anwen. Holding them both steady, he retreated toward his men.

"What's happening?" asked Cerys. The whole tip of the beanstalk was black now, and its trunk was splitting open, disgorging gusts of foul-smelling air and billows of ash. Anwen watched it in horror.

"The magic bean," she said. "I *told* Grandma it was too old to work properly!"

In the field outside Old Stump, the beanstalk was still lush and green, but the crowd at its base was in such an uproar that even Eira was having trouble keeping them in order. Her job was being made especially difficult by Cerys's parents, who were both in near hysterics. Eira couldn't exactly blame them—she was struggling to keep her own anxiety in check.

"Cerys!" howled Mr. Powell, twisting his beard in his fists. "We have to get her back!"

"What if she's being eaten alive as we speak?" said Mrs. Powell. "Oh! Our little angel! Up there all alone with those beasts!"

Eira fixed her with a hard look. "Anwen's up there too, remember."

"What if they're *both* being eaten?" said Mr. Powell.

Eira swallowed the lump of dread that rose in her throat. "They're resourceful girls. We have to trust them to look after each other until we can reach them."

"And how are we going to do that?" demanded Mrs. Powell.

"We'll send some people up to fetch them, of course."

The words were barely out of her mouth when Stillpike bounded forward. "Leave it to me," he said. "The Colonel will rescue those girls in no time." He shouldered his guitar strap, spat on his hands, and scampered to the base of the beanstalk. The monstrous plant was more than eighty feet across now, and its spiraled flanks were ridged and knobbly, giving plenty of handholds.

"What do you think you're playing at, you old fool?" said Meredith. "Even if you make it to the top, the giants will squash you without even noticing."

Stillpike paused. "I may be a humble minstrel, but I'm not about to let those children fend for themselves."

"He's right, Meredith," said Eira. "I'd go up there myself, but I can't manage the climb." She turned to Stillpike. "You're no spring chicken either. Take some people with you, and remember you're just there to get the girls back. Nothing more. Understood?"

"Perfectly," said Stillpike. "Who's with me?" Cerys's parents, and a gaggle of others, hurried forward to join him. "That's the spirit," he said, surveying them with the pride of a general inspecting his troops. He took hold of the nearest leaf and pulled himself up, only to fall flat on his back when it came away in his hands.

"Blast," he said, scrabbling back to his feet. "I don't know my own strength." He tossed the leaf aside, but before it could even hit the ground, it blackened and crumbled away. He blinked in surprise. "Is it supposed to do that?"

"Probably not," said Eira. With a growing sense of foreboding, she looked up the beanstalk's towering trunk. Sure enough, more leaves were shriveling and falling into dust, while the trunk itself was turning black. A fetid stench erupted from the stalk's crumbling flesh, forcing everyone back, their eyes watering. "Get clear, everyone!" she shouted. "The beanstalk is falling!"

People scattered. Eira linked arms with Meredith on one side and Stillpike on the other, and together they broke into a stumbling trot, heading for the field hospital.

"How can it be rotting?" said Meredith. "We only just planted it."

"It's old," Eira panted. "Too old to contain all the magic it needs. It must be burning itself out."

A splintering crack, loud as a clap of thunder, made them all jump. Eira looked over her shoulder and saw that the beanstalk had split from side to side. Clouds of dust spewed from the gap, obscuring the sun. Slowly, with a shuddering moan, the beanstalk leaned toward them.

"Here it comes!" Eira cried. She pulled Meredith and Stillpike to the ground as the trunk broke into a hundred massive pieces, which rained down around them. But wherever they struck the earth they simply burst into plumes of ash, as softly and quietly as feather pillows.

Eira rolled onto her back. It was as though a grubby blizzard had descended on the landscape, coating the fields and trees in a clinging gray blanket. Of the beanstalk, there was nothing left at all.

Stillpike was first to his feet. "No!" he cried, shaking his fist at the sky.

Cerys's parents emerged, coughing and spluttering, from a nearby drift of ash. "Our little sorceress!" said her father. "What are we supposed to do now?"

What indeed? A chill spread through Eira's bones as a sober realization took hold. "There's nothing we *can* do," she said flatly. "That was our only hope of rescuing the girls."

"But it can't be," said Mrs. Powell.

"What about a spell?" said Stillpike. "A potion? Another bean?"

"What other bean?" snapped Eira. "I don't keep a collection."

"We can't just . . ." said Mr. Powell, gesturing helplessly at the gray sky. "I mean, we have to . . ." He sat down heavily, sending up a little cloud of dust, and put his head in his hands. "This is a tragedy."

"It is." Eira got unsteadily to her feet. "And I'm sorry, it's all my fault. Anwen tried to warn me about the bean. I should have listened."

"You did what you could to help everyone," said Meredith, slipping a comforting arm around her. "We'll find a way to fix this."

Eira huffed, but leaned into the hug a little.

A chorus of coughs and splutters was rising from all across the meadow, as people picked themselves up out of the ash. Many of them stood around looking confused, before instinctively drifting back toward the field hospital. Eira watched them go, and sighed. All she wanted was to bring Anwen and Cerys home safe, but there were plenty of people right here who needed her too. She couldn't do it all by herself anymore.

"Stillpike," she said. "There is still one thing you can do to help the girls."

“Name it,” he replied.

“Get to Oldport, as quickly as you can. The town hall there has messenger pigeons. Send one to the capital, to the First Minister’s office, and tell them we need the army.”

His eyebrows shot up. “A military beanstalk?”

She nodded. “I don’t like it, but it’s our only option now.”

“We can take you,” said Mrs. Powell, suddenly hopeful. “Our farm’s not far away. We can have the horse and cart ready in no time.”

“A splendid idea,” said Stillpike. “Let’s get a move on.”

“Excellent,” said Eira. “Meanwhile, Meredith and I will find everyone else some shelter. It’ll be dark in a few hours.”

“I’m right with you,” said Meredith.

The five of them had just started kicking their way through the ashes to the hospital when a series of loud thuds made them turn in surprise. More large blocks were falling to earth, and Eira could see instantly that these weren’t simply the upper vestiges of the beanstalk. They were huge fragments of white stone, and the ground shook as they crashed down.

“What are they?” asked Stillpike, shrinking back in fear.

"They must be falling through the thin place from the Sky Kingdom," said Eira. "It looks like the beanstalk did some damage up there."

They hurried to a safe distance as the pieces rained down, churning up more ash and dust. Through the cloud, Eira was sure she spotted something else fall with them—something that glittered gold and white for an instant, before being obscured by the murk.

Then it was all over, and the birds started singing again.

"That's the third thing to drop out of the sky on us so far today," said Stillpike.

"Let's hope we don't get a fourth," said Eira, shaking the fresh coat of ash from her hair. "Right now, the girls are depending on you, so hurry." She cast a worried look up at the sky.

Hold on, Anwen, she thought. *We'll find a way to reach you both. Just try to keep out of trouble.*

Anwen and Cerys watched in horror as the withered husk of the beanstalk disintegrated and blew away on the breeze. It left behind a gaping hole in the rubble, and, from the vantage point of the Captain's hand,

Anwen could just see down into it. Instead of showing a window into the blue sky of her own world, it was as black and featureless as an old well.

"What have you done?" said Cerys. "You've trapped me here. Forever!"

"Don't blame me!" said Anwen. "I didn't want you along. If you hadn't grabbed hold of me, you'd still be at home."

The mention of home made Cerys's eyes well up. "Mum and Dad," she whimpered. "I'm never going to see them again. And what about the Academy?"

Anwen rolled her eyes at the mention of the Academy, but couldn't keep her own fears at bay. Were either of them ever going to see Old Stump again? "I don't know how we'll get home," she said, "but we'll find some way. This captain seems friendly. Maybe he can help us." She looked up at him, but he was busy addressing his men.

"You, you, and you," he said, nodding to three of the guards. "Set up a perimeter around this hole; I don't want the public stumbling into it by mistake. And if the humans send up another beanstalk, I want to know about it straightaway. Is that clear?"

"Yessir," the three chorused.

"The rest of you, come with me. I'm doubling security in the palace. And as for you two . . ." He looked down at Anwen and Cerys. "You and I have got the hardest job of all."

Anwen's skin prickled with apprehension, and she reached for the sprig of heather in her hair before remembering that she had lost it.

"We're going to tell Princess Flavia that her brother has been murdered," said the Captain.

5

Into the Palace

Anwen's stomach churned with worry as the Captain carried her and Cerys across the square toward the palace. She didn't feel in any physical danger—he held them as delicately as if they were made of glass—but her mind reeled from the revelation that the murdered giant wasn't just rich, he was *royalty*. Not to mention the fact that she and Cerys were trapped here in the Sky Kingdom.

Even more overwhelming was the sheer scale of the giants' world. The black-and-white tiles of the square stretched for almost half a mile in every direction, like a giant chessboard. It was dotted with trees that might have reached the clouds had they been planted in her own world, and the buildings surrounding it glowed pink and ocher in the sunlight.

Giants gathered from all over the square as the Captain passed. Anwen saw their looks of hatred and distrust, and heard the half-muttered comments.

"Disgusting little things."

"*I* certainly wouldn't touch them."

"It's an infestation, that's what it is."

She blushed with shame and anger, and crouched low in the Captain's cupped hand to hide herself from view. Cerys did likewise but, with a muttered incantation, also wrapped herself in a new glamour dress of shimmering white lace. Anwen wished she still had the comfort of her lucky heather, although she couldn't stop her hand wandering to her hair to check for it—it was a nervous reflex. Perhaps Cerys's glamour dress was too.

The palace gates swung open to admit them. The Captain crossed a small parade ground and mounted the steps to the palace doors, where two more guards stood watch.

"Open up," the Captain demanded. "We have important news on the search for King Thibault."

A little thrill ran through Anwen. At last, she had a name to go with the face she had sketched. Thibault. *King* Thibault. Every little bit of information about him was like a piece of a puzzle, and the more pieces she put together, the more real he became. Having a duty to the dead was much easier when you knew who they were.

The doors yawned open. If the outside of the palace was opulent, the inside was spectacular. Golden columns as thick as the beanstalk held up a vaulted ceiling of white marble so high above Anwen's head that it felt like a second sky. Diamond chandeliers the size of upturned oak trees hung from it, casting rainbows of light through the echoing expanse.

This grand hallway was busy with enormous figures whose footsteps rumbled like low thunder: more guards, of course, and a small army of butlers, maids, and other servants. They all looked worried, but paused to watch the Captain as he made his way toward another, more grandiose set of doors at the end of the hall. These were made of solid gold, and Anwen didn't need to be told that they marked the entrance to the throne room.

"Cerys," she gasped. "How do you talk to a princess? Is it 'Your Majesty' or 'Your Royal Highness'? Or just 'ma'am'?"

Cerys put her nose in the air. "I'm not talking to you," she said.

"But we've got to tell the princess what happened to her brother," said Anwen.

"You tell her," Cerys replied. "I'm just going to ask her to send me home."

"How?"

Cerys stiffened. "She must know a way."

Anwen didn't have time to wonder if this was true, as they'd arrived at the glittering doors, where a young man wearing a servant's uniform and a wispy beard was polishing the handles with a piece of cloth. He greeted the Captain with a look of relief.

"There you are, Cato!" He brushed a flop of russet hair from his eyes. "Everyone's frantic. There are all these rumors about a beanstalk, and—" He saw Anwen and Cerys, and backed away so sharply that he bumped into the doors. "It's true!" he said. "The tinies are invading!"

Anwen and Cerys exchanged a look. *Tinies?*

"It's not an invasion, Marcus," the Captain replied. "They're here to see Princess Flavia, and it's urgent."

"You're taking them in there?" Marcus hooked a thumb at the doors. "The Chamberlain won't like that."

"The Chamberlain doesn't like anything," said the Captain, before casting a furtive glance around the hall. "Where is he anyway? He's supposed to be on door duty."

"Maybe he's helping coordinate the search parties," said Marcus. His curiosity was apparently getting the better of him, as he leaned in for a closer look at Anwen and Cerys. "Are you sure these are the only two?" he asked. "I heard they live in packs."

Cerys put her hands on her hips. "We can hear you, you enormous oaf!" she shouted.

Anwen was thankful that her voice was too small to reach Marcus's ears.

"It's just these two," said the Captain. He nodded to the doors. "What's it like in there?"

"Tense," Marcus replied. "I mean, a king isn't supposed to just disappear from his own palace, is he?"

"No," said the Captain gravely. "He's not."

"Personally, I think he's going to come swaggering in tonight as if nothing's happened," said Marcus. "I bet he crept out in disguise to mix with normal people like you and me, and get inspiration for some new songs. That's probably why his lyrics are always so raw and authentic." He developed a bit of a faraway look in his eye. "Yeah, Thibault's out there somewhere, connecting with real life."

Anwen looked up at the Captain, whose face was now ashen.

"He connected with something all right," he said.

Anwen tried to take some calming breaths, but she was too tense. Marcus reached for the handle but was interrupted by the sound of rapidly approaching footsteps.

"Get your hand off that door!"

A small man—at least, small by giant standards, measuring only a hundred feet tall—wearing a shoulder-length periwig to match his neat silver beard, hurried up to them. The look of fury on his face was so strong that Anwen shrank away from him.

"Chamberlain!" Marcus was silenced as the man produced an ornate golden mallet and waved it threateningly in front of Marcus's nose.

"I'm the only one who's allowed to grant access to the throne room, young man. And don't you forget it!"

Marcus tried to retreat, but his back hit the doors again. "I didn't forget," he said, going cross-eyed as the mallet danced in front of him.

"Then who gave you ideas above your station, eh, *Polisher?*"

"I did, Chamberlain," said the Captain.

The Chamberlain swung around, mallet at the ready. Its glittering head was as big as an Old Stump cottage, and it plowed through the air with a low whoosh that was so terrifying, Anwen and Cerys clasped hands without even noticing.

The Chamberlain's rage faltered when he met the Captain's steady gaze. "I should have known," he said. "This is what happens when the palace opens its doors to street urchins like you two. Standards slip."

"Did those standards include staying at your post?" asked the Captain. "You're supposed to be supervising the doors."

Anwen saw a nervous flicker cross the Chamberlain's face, and he slipped a hand beneath his wig to massage his temple. "I was busy with a personal matter," he said. "But never mind that. Why aren't you searching for His Majesty?" The Captain nodded to his cupped hand. When the Chamberlain saw Anwen and Cerys, he went pale. "What," he said, in a deathly whisper, "are *those*?"

"These are . . . ambassadors," the Captain replied. "From the Land Below."

"Out of the question!" said the Chamberlain. "I can't let the kingdom's enemies into the throne room."

"They've found King Thibault," said the Captain. "Do you want to keep the princess waiting?"

The Chamberlain looked shocked, then suspicious. "Surely you don't expect me to believe that His Majesty absconded in the middle of the night to visit the Land Below?"

"It doesn't matter what you believe," said the Captain. "Something terrible's happened, and we need to tell the princess."

The Chamberlain's expression grew even more sour. "Very well," he said. "How am I to announce these creatures?"

"They're girls, not creatures," said the Captain. He smiled reassuringly down at Anwen and Cerys.

"It's a good question, though. I don't actually know your names."

Anwen jumped out of the Captain's palm and scurried up his arm. He went stiff with surprise, but held still as she pulled herself up the gold piping of his uniform onto his shoulder, where she took gentle hold of a curl of black hair that had escaped from beneath his helmet and spoke into his ear. "Can you hear me now?" she asked.

"Loud and clear," he replied.

"Good," said Anwen. "First of all, this Chamberlain is a pompous old windbag."

"Agreed."

"Second, my name is Anwen Sedge, and the girl in your hand is Cerys Powell. We're not really ambassadors. Actually, we didn't mean to come here at all, but there was a bit of an accident with the beanstalk."

"It doesn't matter how you got here," said the Captain. "I just need you to tell Princess Flavia everything you know about what's happened. Can you do that?"

"Yes," said Anwen.

He turned back to the Chamberlain. "Tell the court that Anwen Sedge and Cerys Powell are here to speak with the princess."

"On your own head be it." The Chamberlain raised the mallet and swung it at the gold doors, which rang like a gong, loud enough to make Anwen and Cerys cover their ears. The Chamberlain winced and clutched the side of his head again. *He needs earplugs*, thought Anwen. *Or they need a quieter way to announce people.*

When the sound died away, the Chamberlain shooed Marcus to one side and pushed the doors open. The room beyond shone with polished wood and gold.

"May it please the court to grant an audience to Captain Cato Adami, accompanying Anwen Sludge and Cerys Pile, ambassadors from the Land Below," he announced.

Anwen was too tense to care about the Chamberlain getting her name wrong, and kept tight hold of the Captain's hair, while Cerys sat upright and added a little extra sparkle to her ensemble.

Anwen was just wishing, once again, that her own dress was a little less patched and worn when a woman's voice reached them from the depths of the throne room.

"Proceed."

"Good luck, mate," whispered Marcus. The Captain gave him a nod, and carried Anwen and Cerys across the threshold.

"Your Highness," he said. "I bring terrible news."

6

A Royal Reception

Anwen's eyes struggled to adjust to the shimmering light as she rode on the Captain's shoulder into the throne room. It was a smaller space than the grand hallway, but every bit as lavish—the walls were paneled with cherry-red wood inlaid with gold, and every inch of the room gleamed.

The Chamberlain strode ahead of them, radiating self-importance, and signaled for the Captain to stop as they reached a golden throne on a raised dais. The throne was empty, but the footstool in front of it—as wide as two hay wagons parked end to end—was occupied by a slender female giant, with thick dark hair that spilled over the shoulders of her lilac dress. She held a quill, and she was hunched almost double over a stack of papers in her lap. An expectant crowd of clerks buzzed around her, all bearing more papers, while a page boy in a tricorn hat stood patiently behind her, awaiting orders.

"Captain Cato Adami and . . . guests, ma'am," the Chamberlain proclaimed.

The woman looked up from her work, and Anwen

noticed that the set of her nose and jawline were identical to Thibault's. Not just his sister but his twin, she guessed.

"I hope you're not going to tell me we're at war with the Land Below, Captain," said the princess, dashing her signature onto the topmost paper without looking and handing it to a clerk. "I've got enough problems covering for my layabout brother. Has he turned up yet?"

The Captain cleared his throat nervously. "Yes, Your Highness, but—"

"Good," she said, returning her attention to her work. "Tell him I don't care which dance hall he's ended up in, or how much fun he's having, I need him to get back here and at least try to start acting like a king, while I deal with this beanstalk business. Was there much damage to the monument?"

Anwen felt the muscles in the Captain's shoulder tense beneath her feet.

"I'm sorry, Your Highness," he said. "But your brother is dead."

Silence crashed down on the room in an instant. Very slowly, Princess Flavia laid the quill down. When she looked up again, her face was impassive.

"How?" she asked, very quietly.

"These two girls from the Land Below brought us the news," said the Captain. "Perhaps they'd better explain directly."

Princess Flavia gave a short, jerky nod. Anwen, feeling more self-conscious than ever, hurried down the Captain's arm and pressed her notebook into Cerys's hands. "You do the spell, I'll do the talking," she said. She scrambled up to the Captain's shoulder again, and spoke into his ear. "Can you repeat what I say for the princess?"

"Word for word."

So Anwen recounted everything that had happened in Old Stump, from the moment she had realized a giant was falling from the sky, to her and Cerys's accidental piggyback ride on the beanstalk. She explained about the single wound on Thibault's forehead, and her grandmother's assessment of murder. Cerys cast her projection spell and enlarged Thibault's portrait until it was bigger than life-sized, prompting whispers from the clerks. Princess Flavia stared at it blankly. It was a look that Anwen knew well from her work as a Meadow Witch—news of a sudden death was often too big to take in at once. The princess was in shock.

Sensing that his services were required, the page boy, who appeared to be in his early teens, stepped forward and offered the princess a lace handkerchief. She took it, but held it in her lap.

"And that's why we're here," Anwen finished. "We're very sorry for your loss, Your Highness. All we know for certain is that your brother died somewhere up here in your world, before his body was dropped through the thin place. We don't know who did it, or why, but I'd like to help you investigate the—"

"Help?" barked the Chamberlain, so suddenly that everyone jumped. "For all we know, you lured the king into your world and killed him yourselves, as a preface to an invasion." He swung around to face the princess. "Your Highness, you cannot possibly take these creatures at their word. You should destroy them immediately."

The princess didn't answer. All the color had drained from her face.

"No!" said Anwen, clutching the top of the Captain's ear. "We haven't done anything wrong!"

The Captain grunted in agreement. "In case you've forgotten, Chamberlain, I'm the one in charge of palace security, not you."

"Then I suggest you do a better job," the Chamberlain replied. "Because you let His Majesty disappear from under your nose, and now he's dead."

"Enough!" Princess Flavia shot to her feet, scattering papers everywhere. "Chamberlain. There are protocols to be observed on the death of the king, are there not?" Her voice was taut and trembling.

"Yes, Your Highness," the Chamberlain replied.

"Then go and see to them."

"Of course . . . Your Majesty. Long live the queen!"

As the cry was taken up by the clerks, the Chamberlain retreated to the main doors, shooting a hateful look at Anwen, Cerys, and the Captain as he went. Anwen, emboldened by the Captain's presence, stuck her tongue out at him in response.

As soon as he was gone, Queen Flavia sagged back onto her footstool and put her head in her hands.

"How did this happen, Captain?" she asked through her fingers, while the clerks set about picking up the fallen paperwork.

"I wish I knew, Your Majesty," he replied. "We all saw your brother on his balcony during the concert last night. There were guards posted throughout the palace, including in the hallway leading to his door. They didn't leave their posts all night, he didn't pass any of them, and yet his chambers were empty when the chambermaid arrived to wake him this morning. It's almost like . . ."

"Magic?" Queen Flavia lifted her head and looked squarely at Anwen, whose skin prickled with fear.

"You have to believe me, we had nothing to do with this," she hissed into the Captain's ear. "We'd never even seen a giant before today."

"With all due respect, Your Majesty," said the

Captain, "there's no evidence to suggest these girls were involved."

"Would magic leave any evidence?" the queen asked.

"I . . ." The Captain floundered. "I don't know."

Anwen was about to petition him again when Cerys's voice rang out, loud enough for the whole throne room to hear.

"Of course we didn't do it! You wouldn't even know the king was dead if we hadn't come and told you."

Everyone, including Anwen, stared at her in disbelief.

"How are you doing that?" Anwen called down to her.

"I put the projection spell on my voice, stupid," Cerys replied at the same ringing volume. "I'm sick of you speaking for both of us, while these giants talk about us as if we're not even here."

The clerks cringed, but Cerys rounded on Queen Flavia, unabashed.

"If magic could teleport people from one world to another, we wouldn't have needed a beanstalk, and we wouldn't still be here talking to you. I don't want to invade the Sky Kingdom; I want you to send me home, right now." Her anger spent, she suddenly remembered who she was talking to, and bobbed a curtsy. "I mean, please. Your Majesty."

Anwen wished she'd brought a spare sprig of heather as all eyes turned to the queen, who steepled her long fingers.

"Maybe you are just innocent bystanders," she said. "But I can't send you home immediately."

"Why not?" asked Cerys.

"Because there's no magic in this world, tiny girl. No beanstalks, or flying carpets, or whatever you use where you come from. We'll need something more practical to go down and retrieve the . . ." She faltered for a second. "To retrieve the body." She looked around the room. "Does anyone have any suggestions?"

Nobody spoke, until the page boy stepped forward. "What about a big ladder, Your Majesty?"

A few of the clerks snickered, but the queen snapped her fingers. "Good thinking, Tonino." She pointed to one of the clerks. "You. Notify every ropeyard in the docklands that they're to stop whatever they're working on, and combine forces to make a rope ladder instead. The longest and strongest they've ever made. I want it ready in two days."

The clerk scuttled away, but Cerys looked horrified.

"Two days! I'm supposed to be at the Academy of High Magic by then!"

"If you have a spell to make the job go faster, feel free to use it," said the queen. Cerys hung her head. "I'll take that as a no," the queen continued. "In which case you're going to be staying with us, so I suppose I'd better make you both comfortable. Tonino?"

The page boy snapped to attention. "Your Majesty?"

"I'm putting you in these girls' service," she said. "Ensure they have whatever they need. You can start by going upstairs to the old nursery. You'll find Fame and Fortune Halls under some dust sheets in there somewhere. They should be suitable accommodation."

Tonino's face lit up excitedly. "Yes, ma'am." He dashed away, flashing a huge grin at Anwen and Cerys as he went.

"Captain, I want a permanent guard on the nursery door," said the queen. "The tinies are to remain inside until it's time to send them home."

"Of course, Your Majesty," he replied.

Anwen tapped the top of his ear. "But I could help you find the killer," she said. "I've got a good eye for detail. My grandma said so."

"Thanks," he replied. "But it's for your own safety. The Chamberlain won't be the only one who wants to blame you for what's happened."

Anwen knew this should have chilled her, but she was too frustrated to pay it any mind. "Cerys!" she called. "Tell the queen I can help with the investigation."

"Oh please," said Cerys. "As if you could solve a murder."

Anwen felt as if she had been slapped, and she decided, then and there, that she would show Cerys Powell *exactly* what she could do.

The Captain shifted impatiently, and Anwen had to grip his ear tightly to keep her balance. "That's enough, both of you," he said. "The Chamberlain was right about one thing—the king's murder happened on my watch, so it's my responsibility to bring the killer to justice, not yours." He looked to the queen. "With your permission, ma'am, I'll lock down the palace. Nobody in or out without express written permission from you, or me."

"See that it's done," she replied. "And then?"

"A full sweep of the building, from top to bottom. If we can discover exactly how King Thibault left the palace without being seen, it might lead to other answers. I'd also like to interview every member of staff who was here overnight. We need to know who was where, and when."

Queen Flavia's face tightened, but Anwen could see an uncomfortable emotion squirming just beneath the surface. She couldn't be sure, but it looked like fear.

"Yes," said the queen shortly. "Good. Begin immediately."

At that moment, Tonino reappeared at a brisk trot.

"Your Majesty," he said breathlessly. "I did what you said, but I couldn't find—"

"It doesn't matter," said the queen, rising to her feet. "We all have a lot of work ahead of us." She signaled to the nearest clerk, who handed her the quill and a sheaf of papers. "You're all dismissed."

Anwen looked back as the Captain and Tonino left the throne room. Before the doors closed, she caught a glimpse of the queen immersed in her paperwork, as if nothing had changed. But instead of crouching on the footstool, she now occupied the throne.

Anwen didn't have time to dwell on this, however, as Marcus moved to block the Captain's path.

"Cato!" he said, his eyes wide and fearful. "The Chamberlain's put the whole palace into mourning. Tell me it isn't true!"

The Captain hung his head. "I'm afraid so."

"But . . . but how?"

"That's what I'm going to find out." Very gently, the Captain lifted Anwen from his shoulder and cupped her in his hands alongside Cerys. "Take good care of them, Tonino."

The page boy cupped his own hands, only to see how small they were in comparison to the Captain's. He thought for a moment, then removed his tricorn hat and held it upside down. The Captain lowered the girls into it.

"It's really nice to meet you both," said Tonino, looking down at them with a gap-toothed smile. "My mum used to tell me bedtime stories about the tinies and their magical powers. They were some of my favorites!"

Anwen would have replied, but she couldn't make herself heard without a projection spell, and she had no idea of the right incantation. She certainly wasn't about to ask Cerys for help, so she gave Tonino a perfunctory wave instead.

"Why is the queen sending us to the nursery?" demanded Cerys. "Does she think we're babies?"

"I'm sure you'll like it when you see it," said Tonino.

The Captain clapped Tonino on the shoulder, shaking the hat so badly that Anwen and Cerys fell over each other. "Get them there directly," he said. "I'll check on you all as soon as I can."

Anwen disentangled herself from Cerys, making sure to get a few digs in with her elbows as she did so.

"Clumsy twit," snapped Cerys.

"Is everything all right?" asked Tonino.

"Everything's fine," Anwen grumbled to herself. But that was a lie, and she knew it. There was a killer on the loose, and, as Tonino set off through the palace, Anwen had only one thought in her head: *What if they strike again?*

7

Fortune Hall

The palace was even bigger than Anwen had imagined. She propped her elbows on the upturned brim of Tonino's hat, and stared in wonder as he carried her and Cerys up winding staircases, along cavernous hallways, and through rotundas sparkling with stained glass. As the Captain had explained in the throne room, there were guards stationed everywhere, and it made her wonder how King Thibault could possibly have vanished from the palace without being seen.

"I hope you're enjoying this," muttered Cerys, who sat in the bottom of the hat, looking glum.

"Yes, thanks," said Anwen. "You should come up and take a look instead of sulking about the Academy."

Cerys pulled her glamour dress a little tighter around herself, and said nothing.

They passed another pair of guards and entered a curved hallway with doors along both sides. Most of them were painted white, but Tonino stopped at one painted a deep forest green.

"Here we are," he said. "The royal nursery."

Anwen gasped as he carried them inside. The room was flooded with late afternoon sunlight, which streamed in through floor-to-ceiling windows. The ceiling was painted to resemble a summer sky, with white puffs of cloud and birds in flight, while the walls were covered in a mural of a lush forest overgrown with ferns, mosses, and flowers. Anwen saw the painted faces of woodland creatures peeping out from between the trunks. She felt she was really standing in a forest clearing, and she liked it immediately.

In the center of the clearing was the grandest dollhouse that Anwen had ever seen. In the human world, it would have been a mansion—four stories tall, and nearly eighty feet wide. Real glass winked in its windows, and a gold filigree sign above the door read FORTUNE HALL.

"I hope it's comfortable enough for you," said Tonino, setting his hat down gently in front of the dollhouse. "I think it was one of Queen Flavia's toys when she was a little girl."

Cerys came alive at the sight of the house and elbowed Anwen aside in her haste to reach it. "Is this where we're staying?" She still had the projection spell on her voice, which rang out loud enough for Tonino to hear.

"As long as you don't mind sharing," he replied.

"King Thibault's old dollhouse is supposed to be here too, but I can't find it anywhere."

Cerys looked almost as appalled as Anwen felt. "You want me to share a room with *her*?"

Tonino fumbled with a hidden catch, and opened the front of the house like the covers of a book. "No," he said. "Just the house."

Anwen was speechless—every room of Fortune Hall was perfectly detailed and furnished. There was a drawing room, a kitchen, a dining room, and a sweeping staircase leading to a whole suite of bedrooms and a study. There was even a bathroom, with twin washbasins and a claw-foot tub.

Cerys dashed into the open frontage, taking the stairs two at a time. Anwen, meanwhile, rushed into the dining room, marveling at every detail. The table was laid with a silk cloth, real glass goblets, and gold cutlery, all of them at perfect human scale. Bone china plates were piled high with ceramic fruit, so exquisitely painted that it almost looked real.

"There are clothes in these wardrobes!" came Cerys's voice from upstairs. "Can we wear them?"

"Go ahead," Tonino replied. "Her Majesty told me to give you everything you need, after all."

"Wonderful!" said Cerys. "Maybe Anwen will finally find something that makes her look good."

Anwen smoothed down her woolen dress. "I look fine, thank you," she muttered.

While they busied themselves exploring their surroundings, Tonino lay down on the moss-green carpet and propped his chin on his hands. "How come I can hear one of you, but not the other?" he asked.

"That's a good question" came Cerys's voice. "Perhaps Anwen can explain. Oh no, that's right! She doesn't know how to put a projection spell on her voice, because that's High Magic, and she can only use common or garden Folk Magic, the poor thing."

Anwen knew she was being goaded, but she stormed upstairs into the master bedroom, where Cerys had emptied the contents of several large wardrobes onto the four-poster bed and was now sorting through them, holding each item against herself in front of a full-length mirror.

"I can be just as good at High Magic as you," Anwen declared.

Cerys paused her fashion show. "Then I'm sure you won't have any trouble proving it."

"Maybe I will." Anwen put her fingertips to her throat, closed her eyes, and tried to picture the shift in reality she needed. It was hard to keep it in focus, though—she had never tried a projection spell before, and wasn't entirely certain what it required. When she thought she finally had it, she whispered the words she guessed would take the idea from her imagination into reality. "Siarad yn anferth."

She heard the snap of the spell making itself real, and felt a promising tingle in her throat. She turned an imperious look on Cerys, only to find that she was rocking back and forth with laughter.

"Go ahead and say something," said Cerys. "I can't wait to hear it."

Anwen's face flushed. "You don't know what—" she started, and immediately clamped her hand over her mouth. Her voice was louder all right, but it was halfway between a strangled croak and a phlegmy cough.

Cerys hooted with laughter. "You sound like a frog trying to vomit," she said. "Go on, say something else."

"No!" Anwen replied, before she could stop herself. It came out sounding like a wet belch. Her cheeks glowing red, she hastily canceled the spell.

Tonino looked awkward. "I'm sure this High Magic stuff must be really difficult," he said. "Maybe you just need more practice."

Anwen turned away so that neither of them would see her wipe away a tear of embarrassment. "Yeah," she said. "Maybe."

There was a knock at the nursery door, and a footman entered, carrying a silver tray as wide as Farmer Pebin's barn. Two steaming plates of food sat on it.

"From the royal kitchen," he said, placing the tray on the floor beside Tonino's upturned hat. "Her Majesty specified two small portions."

Anwen looked down onto a roast quail that was bigger than she was, lying on a bed of spinach leaves, accompanied by caramelized grapes as big as melons. She gave a delighted laugh. "That's enough to feed everyone in Old Stump for a month."

"Two months," said Cerys, casting a silk ball gown aside.

The footman looked at them as if they had crawled out from under a rock, but left without a word. Before the door swung shut behind him, Anwen had time to see that a guard had taken up a position in the hallway outside.

To keep unwanted people out, or to keep us in? she wondered, before deciding it was probably both.

She clattered downstairs behind Cerys and out onto the carpet. It was like walking through spongy, ankle-deep grass, but it didn't take them long to reach the dinner plates. The quail radiated heat like ovens, and the rich, sweet smell of cooked meat filled Anwen's nostrils. She hadn't realized how famished she was until now.

"This is almost worth being stuck here," said Cerys. She climbed onto the rim of the nearest plate, picked up a caramelized grape in both hands, and sank her teeth into it. "Ish sho good," she said.

Anwen headed for the other plate. The quail was still too hot to touch, so she contented herself with a single spinach leaf, almost two feet wide. She rolled it into a tube and took a big bite out of the end. It was fresh, crisp and crunchy. She crammed another mouthful between her lips, and let out a contented burp.

"Pig," said Cerys, spraying flecks of grape everywhere. Anwen shot her a look that could have curdled milk, and wished she could summon every bird in the Sky Kingdom to smother Cerys in droppings. But she had a better idea than petty revenge—she was going to prove Cerys wrong.

She tucked the remains of the leaf under her arm, hopped off the plate, and climbed into the crook of Tonino's elbow.

"You want to come up?" he said, and lifted her onto his shoulder.

"Do you mind if I ask you some questions?" she said into his ear.

"Go ahead," he replied. "I've got lots of questions for you too. Like, is it true that everyone in the Land Below flies around on broomsticks?"

Anwen laughed. "No. Most of us walk if we want to get somewhere, although the rich ride horses."

"Oh." He sounded disappointed. "If I had magic, I'd use it to go everywhere, just like in the stories."

Anwen suspected that the giants' stories about humans were as heavily embellished as Stillpike's fireside tales of giants. "That's not really how it works," she said. "Not many people in our world can actually use magic. Most of us are just like you giants."

"Giants?" Tonino chuckled, forcing Anwen to grab his collar as his shoulders shook. "We're normal-sized, and you're just tiny. No offense."

"None taken," said Anwen.

"So, what do you want to ask me?" said Tonino.

After a few seconds' consideration, Anwen decided on the direct approach. "Who do you think murdered King Thibault?"

Tonino's smile faded quickly. "I wish I knew."

"He didn't have any enemies?" asked Anwen.

Tonino blinked. "The public loved him."

She took another bite of the spinach leaf and crunched thoughtfully as she tried to imagine what her grandmother would do.

Don't just listen to what he says, came Eira's voice from her subconscious. *Listen to what he* doesn't *say*.

Anwen suddenly knew what her next question had to be. "What did *you* think of him?"

She could only see a little of Tonino's face from where she stood, but it was enough to make out his twitch of discomfort. "It doesn't matter what I thought," he replied. "He was the king, and I'm just a page boy."

Cerys looked up from the remaining half of her grape. "What is a page boy anyway?" she asked.

"I help Queen Flavia with all her little daily tasks," he said. "Getting her clothes ready, carrying things, relaying messages, that sort of stuff. She's a busy woman."

Anwen thought back to their arrival in the throne room, and the sight of Flavia sitting on her brother's footstool, swamped with paperwork. What was it she had called Thibault? *A layabout* . . . "Did she often end up doing Thibault's work for him?" she asked.

Tonino's look of discomfort was practically a grimace this time. "You have to understand, Thibault wasn't very good at the behind-the-scenes stuff," he said. "All the paperwork and legal jargon just made him frustrated, so he ignored it. But he was really good with people." He paused. "Mostly. At least, he was when he was playing his music."

"He was a musician?" said Anwen.

"The most popular musician in the whole kingdom," Tonino replied. "People came from all over to hear him perform."

Anwen remembered something the Captain had said in the throne room, about the last time Thibault had been seen. "Did he perform here at the palace last night?" she asked. "On a balcony?"

"Yes, the one outside his bedroom, overlooking the piazza," said Tonino. "There were thousands of us watching."

"You were there?"

"Of course," said Tonino. "Actually, Thibault *ordered* most of the palace staff to attend, but it was still better than work." He smiled. "Someone bought me a toffee apple."

Cerys groaned and tossed the last of her grape aside. "I'm sure this is all very interesting, or at least it would be if I could hear more than half the conversation. Honestly, Anwen, if you can't project your voice properly, the polite thing would be to stop talking."

"Then it's just as well I wasn't talking to you," Anwen shouted down to her.

Cerys gave a dismissive shrug. "I'm stuffed," she said. "I might come back for more of this later, but right now I'm going to try on some clothes and have a little nap."

"I'll close the house up for you," said Tonino. He let Anwen slide down his arm onto the carpet, then got up and shut the front of Fortune Hall.

"I'll let you know if I need anything else," said Cerys. With a flick of her hair, she opened the front door and stepped inside.

Anwen was just about to make a very rude gesture in the direction of the dollhouse when a piercing scream tore through the room. Tonino jumped, making the ground shake, and Cerys burst out of Fortune Hall again, her eyes wide with fright.

"What was that?" she cried.

"It came from somewhere down the hall," said Anwen. A moment later, they heard several pairs of running feet pass the nursery door.

Tonino made toward it. "Wait here," he said. "I'll find out what's happening."

"You can't leave us," said Cerys. "What if it's the murderer on the loose?"

Tonino dithered. "There's a guard outside," he said. "And I'll only be a minute." He seized the doorknob before putting his other hand to his head. "My hat!" He dashed back, picked it up from the floor, and placed it, very precisely, on his head. "The Chamberlain would be furious if he saw me without it," he explained. "Be right back!"

He slipped out, leaving Cerys to glower after him. "I don't think that's a good idea, do you?" she said. But Anwen didn't reply, and when Cerys looked around, she realized she was entirely alone.

Anwen crouched in the upturned brim of Tonino's hat, trying not to be sick—he had broken into a run, and the bounding motion was making her queasy. She had a giant's-eye view of the hallway rushing past over the edge of the brim, and she was thankful when he finally stopped at a group of servants clustered outside an open door. She ducked lower, hoping not to be seen.

"Are you sure this is where it came from?" asked one of the servants.

"It sounded like it," said another. "But these are the king's chambers. They're supposed to be empty."

Anwen's skin prickled. Thibault's rooms! The last place he was seen alive before his disappearance. Surely there had to be some answers inside? She was wondering how she could go about getting to them when a guard waded into the crowd, pushing everyone back from the door.

"Clear the hallway," he ordered.

"Someone's inside," said Tonino. "We all heard the scream. They might need help."

"They'll get it when backup arrives," the guard replied. "Right now, I need everyone to go about their business." He spread his arms and tried to herd the group away.

Frustration gnawed at Anwen as Tonino turned back in the direction of the nursery. How was she going to find her answers now? But while the guard was focused on the rest of the group, Tonino slipped behind the man's back and through the open door.

Anwen could scarcely believe her luck. Tonino was clearly pluckier than he seemed.

He stepped into a spacious foyer hung with silks. Anwen heard sobbing coming from a doorway to their right and, as Tonino crept toward it, a horrible thought occurred to Anwen—what if Cerys was right and the killer had struck again?

Every muscle in her body tensed as Tonino pushed open the door.

8

One Lump or Two?

Anwen peered over the brim of Tonino's hat, bracing herself for a scene of blood and devastation as he stepped out of the foyer and into Thibault's bedroom. What she saw instead was a neat and tidy room, about the same size as the nursery, with three large windows in the outer wall. A huge bed took up much of the space, but Anwen's attention was drawn to a golden guitar, propped on a stand opposite the windows. It was inlaid with mother-of-pearl, and the head was shaped like a woman's face, with flowing hair and mouth open, as if in song.

A matronly, gray-haired chambermaid sat on the edge of the bed, wringing her hands together and sniffling.

"Gabriela!" said Tonino, hurrying to her side. "What's wrong?"

Anwen crouched lower as Gabriela blinked at Tonino through her tears.

"I . . . I came in to finish up yesterday's bedding," said Gabriela. "There was no sign of it when I arrived to wake up His Royal Nibs this morning . . . I mean, His Majesty, may he rest in peace."

"Is that all?" said Tonino. "Don't worry, I'm sure we can find it together."

"You don't understand," said Gabriela. "This isn't about the bedding."

She pointed with a trembling finger at the rear wall. It was taken up by a tightly packed bookcase, a wardrobe, and some shelves bearing vases, sculptures, and other ornaments. Lying on its side on the floor below one of the shelves was a golden bust.

Gabriela took a shuddering breath. "That was on the shelf, but it was facing the wall, instead of into the room."

"So?" said Tonino.

"So?" she replied in horror. "You know what His Majesty was like—everything had to be perfect, or my job was on the line. I know he's not with us anymore, but I suppose it's become habit. I picked up the bust to turn it around and . . . and then . . ." Her voice broke.

Tonino approached the bust carefully, and Anwen had a good view of it as he picked it up. She wasn't terribly surprised to see that it was a model of Thibault himself—the high cheekbones and strong chin were identical to those she had sketched in Old Stump, although the bust showed his hair fashioned into a huge pompadour. A pompadour, the tip of which was stained with dried blood.

Anwen clasped her hands together in a mixture of revulsion and excitement. *The murder weapon!*

Tonino dropped the bust and backed away in shock. "Someone needs to fetch Captain Adami," he said.

"They already did." The Captain strode into the room, and Anwen dropped flat behind the brim of the hat. She held her breath as the Captain's footsteps crossed to the bust.

"Who found this?" he asked.

"I did," said Gabriela.

"Gabby." The Captain's voice softened. "I want you to tell me all about it. But first, Tonino, you're not supposed to be here."

"I'm sorry, Captain," said Tonino. "I just came in to make sure everything was all right, but . . ." To Anwen's surprise, he began swaying on his feet, rocking her as if she was on board a ship in heavy seas. "Sorry, the sight of blood makes me queasy. I think . . . I think I'm going to be sick!"

"Not in here, it's a crime scene!" said the Captain. "Go outside and get some air."

Tonino let out a low groan and rushed to the

windows. One of them doubled as a glass door, and he opened it onto a wide balcony overlooking the parade ground in front of the palace. Before Anwen could react, he snatched his hat off his head and turned it upside down, ready to catch the contents of his stomach. Horrified and helpless, she slipped out from under the brim and plunged toward the parade ground, six hundred feet below. Her guts lurched up into her throat, and terror made everything move in slow motion. Perhaps that was why she was able to grab the lace of Tonino's cuff at the last possible second, leaving her dangling over empty space by one hand.

"Help!" she screamed.

Tonino felt the tug on his sleeve, looked down, and sprang back from the balustrade. "Anwen!" He dropped the hat and scooped her up in his other hand, cradling her against his chest. "My goodness! Are you all right?"

She trembled in his palm, too shocked to speak, but managed a shaky nod.

"I'm so sorry!" he said. "I thought you were still in the nursery. How did you even get here?" He lifted her to his ear, but she had to take a few deep breaths before she could get the words out.

"I stowed away in your hat," she said.

He looked at her in disbelief. "Why?"

She considered concocting some excuse, but her scattered thoughts weren't up to it. Nor did she like the idea of lying, especially after he had just saved her life. "I'm investigating King Thibault's murder," she said.

"But the Captain said you weren't allowed."

And Cerys said I wasn't capable, Anwen thought, but instead she said, "He doesn't have to know. And I'm here now. I thought, where there's screaming, there might be clues."

"It looks like you were right," he said.

They both glanced back through the window, but the Captain was now sitting beside Gabriela, his back to them, as she recounted her experience with the bust, complete with dramatic gestures and lengthy pauses to dab at her eyes with a handkerchief.

"Do you think someone killed Thibault with that bust?" asked Tonino.

"I'm sure of it," Anwen replied. "One strong blow to the head. Which means he didn't sneak out of the palace before he died. It happened right here, inside his own room."

Tonino shuddered, and it felt like a small earthquake. "But that's worse!" he said. "It means the killer was able to get past all the palace security."

The realization made Anwen's skin prickle with dread. Tonino was right—if the killer could strike here, then nobody in the palace was safe.

"We don't have long before the Captain comes to check on me," said Tonino. "What can I do to help?"

Anwen thought quickly. "I need to get a few basic facts straight," she said. "Is this the balcony where Thibault held his concert last night?"

"Yes," he replied. "He came out of his room with his guitar, stood here, and played and sang for a couple of hours."

"What time was this?"

"He started at ten o'clock and played until midnight," said Tonino. "Although it started getting cold at eleven, so he went back into his room and finished the last half of the concert from there."

Anwen could feel the cool evening breeze against her face already, as the westering sun kissed the city's gilded rooftops. "How could you hear him play if he was inside?"

"He opened all the balcony windows," said Tonino. "We couldn't see him, but we could still hear everything."

Anwen's mind fizzed as it digested all this new information. She had no idea if any of it was useful, but it gave her a fuller picture of Thibault's final movements.

She looked over the edge of the balcony. Beyond the parade ground and its wrought iron fence, the piazza stretched out like a vast plain, with the hill of the shattered memorial in its center. A ring of guards stood watch around it, keeping away the streams of people heading to the palace gates, where a sizable crowd had gathered. Those at the front were tying flowers, wreaths, and handwritten notes to the ironwork. Many of the people wore black and, even from this height, Anwen could see tearful faces pointed in their direction.

"Thibault really had a lot of fans," she said.

"He was a star before he became king," said Tonino.

"Gabriela didn't sound too keen," she replied.

Tonino's eyes flicked back to the bedroom, where Gabriela was being escorted out by a sympathetic guard, while the Captain surveyed the bust again. "She had to clean up after him every day," he said. "I think it was quite a tough job."

A slob as well as a layabout, thought Anwen, logging this fact for later reference. "We should go," she said. "Can I get back in your hat?"

"You'll be safer in my pocket," he replied, tugging open the breast pocket of his waistcoat, which contained a neatly folded lace handkerchief. It was a perfect fit, and the handkerchief a useful shield—she could see out through the lace without being spotted herself. Tonino's heartbeat thrummed like a gigantic drum against her back, steady and reassuring.

"Feeling better?" asked the Captain as Tonino stepped back inside.

"Yes, thank you," he replied. "I just needed a moment."

As they spoke, Anwen took the opportunity to sneak a better look at Thibault's bedroom. There was a nightstand beside the bed with a glass of water, a few jars of what looked like face cream, and a thick book with the title *Crop Rotation: A History*.

At least he was well-read, she supposed. *But what an odd choice of topic.*

Tonino made for the bedroom door. At the same time, the Captain replaced the bust on its shelf, facing the wardrobe, and Anwen saw it in profile for the first time. There was something on its side, above the left ear. It was small and dark and speckled, but it was unmistakable—a second bloodstain.

Her thoughts raced as Tonino carried her out of Thibault's chambers and back into the hallway, where a pair of guards now stood watch outside the door.

There was just one wound on Thibault's body, which meant he had only been struck once with the bust.

So where had the second bloodstain come from?

9

Pieces of the Puzzle

"Where have you been?" demanded Cerys as Tonino lifted Anwen out of his pocket and set her down in front of Fortune Hall. "You abandoned me!" She had swapped her glamour dress, and the tattered rags underneath it, for jade silk pajamas, and her magically amplified voice filled the room.

"We were in the king's chambers, looking for clues," said Tonino.

"And we found plenty," added Anwen smugly.

Cerys looked at her with disdain. "Don't tell me you're serious about catching the killer," she said.

"Don't worry, Tonino and I are managing just fine without you," Anwen replied.

She breezed past Cerys without a second glance, making for the plate of roast quail. She knew that the only thing Cerys hated more than being insulted was being ignored. She peeled off a long strip of baked, crispy quail skin and, sure enough, before she had taken her second bite, Cerys was beside her.

"So what did you find? Not that I care."

"Nothing that would interest you," said Anwen, enjoying Cerys's look of suppressed anger.

"Tonino, tell me!" said Cerys.

"King Thibault was beaten to death in his bedroom, with a gold bust of himself," Tonino replied. "Imagine being killed with your own face!" He stuck his tongue out in disgust. "The bust was covered in blood."

"Too much blood," said Anwen, around another mouthful of quail. "Two bloodstains on the bust, but only one wound on Thibault's body. So where did the second bloodstain come from?"

Cerys cocked an eyebrow. "Perhaps you just can't count."

Before Anwen could reply, the nursery door opened and the Chamberlain strode in. He wore a black armband, and was followed by a trio of servants, carrying a folding screen between them.

"What's happening?" asked Tonino.

"The palace has entered a period of official mourning," said the Chamberlain. "Put this on immediately." He produced another armband from inside his robes. As Tonino slipped it over his sleeve, a second group of servants entered, carrying a folding bed, a small chest, and a stack of neatly folded clothes.

"Hey, those are my things," said Tonino.

"You are to be at the disposal of these tinies night and day," said the Chamberlain. He motioned to the servants, who placed Tonino's belongings in one corner of the room and erected the screen in front of them.

Meanwhile, the Chamberlain patrolled the room, examining every shelf and surface closely. He swiped a finger across a toy chest, and it came up coated in dust. "When was this room last cleaned?"

"The nursery's not used anymore, sir," one of the servants replied. "The maids only tend to it once a month."

The Chamberlain dusted his finger with a handkerchief. "Unacceptable. Go and fetch a cleaning team."

The servants all hurried away. The Chamberlain followed, but paused in the doorway.

"I apologize that the room wasn't up to the standards you deserve," he said, his face a mask of contempt. "The oversight will be rectified shortly. Good day." With a swish of his robe, he was gone.

"He's very strange," said Cerys. "Does he hate us or not?"

"He hates everyone," Tonino replied. "Don't take it personally."

"It's hard not to when he told the queen to kill us," said Cerys. "But now he's worried about our room being dusty. I don't understand."

"It's his job to uphold palace standards," said Tonino. "You're official guests, which means he has to treat you with respect, no matter what he thinks of you."

Cerys's eyes sparkled. "Does that mean we can boss him around?"

Tonino's face lit up. "Oh yeah! Probably!"

"No," said Anwen. "We can't afford any trouble if we're going to investigate Thibault's murder."

"If *you're* going to investigate it, you mean," said Cerys. "I just want to stay in Fortune Hall and live like royalty until we go home. Anyway, we've been in nothing but trouble since we got here."

"Which is why I don't want to cause any more," Anwen replied. "Let everyone think we're harmless."

"We *are* harmless!"

"Exactly."

Tonino, who had been watching the exchange like a tennis match, sighed so heavily his outrush of breath tousled their hair. "I really wish I could hear you both," he said. "Are you sure there's no way to make that spell work on your voice, Anwen?"

She shifted uncomfortably, the memory of her last embarrassment still raw. "I suppose I could give it another go."

"Please don't," said Cerys. "My ears couldn't take it."

"Then what do you suggest?" Anwen demanded.

Cerys arched an eyebrow. "I might be willing to do it for you."

"What's the catch?" asked Anwen.

"Nothing much," Cerys replied. "Just admit that you're hopeless at High Magic."

"No."

"Admit it, or I won't do it."

Anwen fought down a simmering mix of embarrassment and anger. "I'm not good enough at High Magic to do the spell properly," she said. "I'd like you to show me."

"Say please."

Anwen bared her teeth. "Please."

Cerys smiled at her the way a shark might. "That's all I wanted to hear," she said, and leaned over to touch Anwen's neck. "Siaradwch gyda chryfder."

Anwen felt the magic settle in her throat. "Thank you," she said. The words broke out of her with satisfying power.

"Hey, I can hear you!" said Tonino. "Fantastic."

"You're welcome, Anwen," said Cerys. "But next time you'll have to do it yourself."

"Just watch me," said Anwen.

Tonino sat down cross-legged in front of them. "How does all this magic stuff work anyway?" he asked. "I still don't understand it."

"It's simple really," said Cerys. "There's High Magic, which is complex spells practiced by professionals, and Folk Magic, which is simple stuff for hobbyists."

"That's not true, and you know it," said Anwen. "It's more like . . ." She cast around for an example, and hit upon the plates of food. "It's more like a meal. High Magic is a formal banquet. There's a lot of etiquette to follow, and the recipes—or the spells—are very precise. Oh, and most of the people involved are rich."

"I'm not rich," said Cerys. "I'm just brilliant."

Anwen ignored her. "Folk Magic is a meal between friends, cooked in a farmhouse kitchen, with a few homegrown ingredients," she continued. "You can improvise the recipes, as long as the results work."

Tonino licked his lips. "Both of those sound good," he said. "Or maybe I'm just hungry."

Anwen regarded the pile of food in front of her. "You might as well help yourself to this," she said. "There's no way we're going to eat it all."

Tonino shook his head. "Servants aren't allowed to eat food for guests," he said. "And we're definitely not allowed to eat abovestairs."

"That's a stupid rule," said Cerys. "And Anwen's right, this will all go to waste if you don't have any."

Tonino looked nervously toward the nursery door. "Maybe while the Chamberlain's not around . . ." He nudged the grapes away from the rest of the food. "I've never liked grapes," he said as he twisted a drumstick off the quail and took a dainty bite from it. When nobody burst into the room to reprimand him, he took another, bigger bite, and chewed happily for a moment before asking, "So, Cerys, you do High Magic, and Anwen does Folk Magic?"

"Yes," said Cerys. "I'm going to the Academy of High Magic when I get home, to train as a glamourist. In a few years, I'll be able to create the finest illusions anyone's ever seen."

"What will you do with them?" asked Tonino.

"I want to work in the theater, creating magical costumes and effects," she said. "Imagine a storm scene with boiling clouds overhead and waves crashing off the stage that look so real you can almost feel the salt spray on your skin."

Tonino grinned. "That sounds amazing."

"My dream is to create a whole room out of glamour magic," Cerys continued. "So people think they're in a forest like this one, or at the bottom of the ocean, or . . . or anywhere they want to be."

For a few seconds, even Anwen was lured into Cerys's fantasy, and she pictured the painted animals on the nursery walls springing into life. How wonderful that would be. Then she remembered whose idea it was, and shoved the image to the back of her mind. "Very fancy, but not very useful," she said.

"All right then, clever clogs," said Cerys. "Tell us about your oh-so-interesting life as a ditch witch."

"As a what?" said Tonino.

"She thinks she's being funny," said Anwen. "I'm training to be a Meadow Witch, like my grandma. We use Folk Magic to help people with all their day-to-day problems. Finding lost objects, painkillers for toothaches, spells to keep winter drafts out of their houses. And we're a farming community, so there's a lot of talking to animals, which I enjoy."

"That sounds great too," said Tonino.

"It's all right, I suppose," she said. "But I want to do bigger and better things."

Tonino stripped the last of the meat from the drumstick. "Like what?"

Anwen paused. "Study transfiguration at the Academy," she said. "Or maybe elemental magic, I haven't decided yet."

Tonino's great brow furrowed a little. "Sounds good," he replied. "What would you use them for?"

Anwen opened her mouth to reply, then realized she didn't have a good answer for him.

At that instant, the nursery door opened, and Tonino leapt to his feet.

"I wasn't eating!" he said, wiping the juices from his chin with his sleeve. But the Chamberlain was nowhere in sight. Instead a couple of maids and Marcus, the polisher, filed in past the watchful eye of the guard. They all stared with open curiosity at Anwen and Cerys.

"Hello, Marcus," said Anwen, waving.

He looked surprised to hear her speak, but tugged his forelock. "Don't mind us, miss," he said. "The Chamberlain's asked us to give the room a going over."

As they set about dusting and polishing, Anwen realized they might be able to help move her investigation forward.

"Were any of you at King Thibault's concert last night?" she asked. "Cerys and I are so sorry we'll never get to hear him play, but we'd love to hear all about it."

The servants exchanged nervous glances.

"Aye, we were all there," said the older of the two maids. "As ordered."

"He must have sounded wonderful," said Anwen. "How many band members were playing with him?"

"Oh, His Majesty never performed with anyone

else," the other maid replied. "He wouldn't even let anyone near his guitar. Except Marcus here, of course."

Marcus looked up from shining the gold catches on the windows. "That's right," he said. "I'm the official polisher of the royal guitar. Well, not officially official, but I'm the only person he trusted to do it."

"Wow," said Tonino. "I saw him fire servants just for looking at it too closely."

"I think it helped that he knew I was a fan," said Marcus.

This was the sort of insight that Anwen had been hoping for. "You liked his music?" she asked.

"Loved it," Marcus replied. "I know he wasn't an easy man to get along with, but I play a bit of guitar myself, so I know real skill when I hear it. I never missed a performance."

"It sounds like he didn't let you," said Cerys.

"I had to be there anyway, to shine the guitar before he went in front of the public," said Marcus. "He always had to look his best."

Anwen tried not to look too eager. "Did you shine his guitar before the concert last night?" she asked.

"Of course," said Marcus.

"Tell me all about it."

Marcus moved to a nearby chest of drawers and

began polishing the wood. "There's not much to tell," he said. "I arrived at his chambers at about five to ten and polished the guitar while he finished doing his hair. Then I handed the guitar over, he thanked me, and I left to join the crowd in the piazza."

"Oh yes!" Tonino piped up. "You're the one who bought me the toffee apple!"

"Was that you?" Marcus smiled. "You're welcome. They were always my favorite when I was a kid."

Anwen, who had been hoping for some big revelation, deflated slightly. "Did you notice anything unusual in Thibault's room?" she asked. "Was anyone else there?"

"You sound like Cato, asking all these questions," said Marcus. "But no, we were alone. Thibault even locked the door behind me when I left, so he wouldn't be disturbed." He wrung his chamois leather in his hands. "I can't believe I'll never hear him play again."

Everyone in the room shared a moment of solemn silence, which ended abruptly as the Chamberlain entered.

"Well?" he snapped. "If you've finished in here, you have other duties to attend to." He shooed them out of the room before taking a last, critical look around. "Tolerable," he said, then winced and put a hand to his head.

"Are you all right, sir?" asked Tonino.

The Chamberlain snatched his hand from his face. "I'm fine," he snapped. "Good night."

Only when he had pulled the door shut behind him did Anwen realize that the sun had dipped out of sight, and the long shadows in the room were spreading into an inky darkness.

"Perhaps we should get some sleep," said Tonino. "It's been a busy day." He crossed to the windows and drew the heavy drapes, then lit a small lantern and placed it on the chest of drawers. The warm glow flickered, pushing the shadows back.

But Anwen was too alert to be tired, and she sat down and opened her notebook. "You sleep if you want to," she said, readying her stick of charcoal. "But I'm tired of this case giving us nothing but questions. It's time to put some of the pieces together, and get some answers."

10
Casebook

Anwen, Cerys, and Tonino sat together around the lamp as the dusky shadows deepened in the corners of the nursery.

"Here's what we know so far," said Anwen, turning to a clean page in her notebook. "King Thibault held a concert last night, between ten o'clock and midnight. He spent the first hour outside on his balcony, then performed the last half from inside his bedroom. So we know he was still alive at midnight."

"Oh yes," said Tonino. "It was definitely him playing and singing the whole time."

Anwen underlined the times, then began a new paragraph. "Thibault's body was dropped onto Old Stump at noon today, and my grandma reckoned he'd been dead for at least twelve hours. That means the killer must have struck as soon as the concert ended."

"Gosh," said Tonino. "It probably happened while we were all heading back inside, and we had no idea."

"You didn't hear a struggle?" asked Anwen.

"No, nothing," he replied.

Anwen kept writing. "Marcus was in the bedroom

to polish the guitar a few minutes before the concert," she said. "According to him, Thibault was alone, and locked the door before the concert. We need to find out what changed."

"Simple," said Cerys. "The concert ended, Thibault unlocked the door, then someone went in and whacked him over the head."

"We don't know for certain that he did unlock the door," said Anwen. "Even if he did, it doesn't explain how the killer got past the guards at the end of the hallway, or how they smuggled Thibault's body out of the palace. Come to think of it, why did they move Thibault's body at all?"

"To hide it," said Tonino. "Before you two got here, we all thought Thibault had just snuck out to a party somewhere. He's done it before."

Anwen remembered Marcus telling Captain Adami his theory that Thibault had left the palace in disguise, searching for inspiration for new songs. "Maybe," she said. "But in that case, why leave the murder weapon behind?"

"Perhaps the killer was in a hurry," said Cerys.

Anwen shook her head. "No, whoever did this was very careful to avoid being spotted. They wouldn't overlook a detail that obvious." She wrote MURDER WEAPON in her notebook and underlined it. It was a gap in the puzzle, and it frustrated her. If the killer had left the murder weapon behind, it meant they weren't trying to disguise the fact that Thibault had died in his bedroom. But then why go to such lengths to move the body? The two facts didn't fit together.

"Then there's the second bloodstain, on the side of the bust," said Anwen. "That suggests two blows with the murder weapon, but Thibault was only struck once."

The three of them pondered this point in silence for a moment.

"What if he fought back?" asked Tonino. "He could have used the bust to defend himself, before being overpowered and killed."

"Which means the second bloodstain must belong to the killer," said Anwen. "It's a good theory. If we can find someone with a nasty wound, we might have found our murderer."

"It's the Chamberlain," said Cerys. "What? Don't look at me like that, you both saw him grab his head just now. And he did it before, outside the throne room."

It's certainly possible, Anwen thought. "But why would he kill Thibault?" she asked. "What's his motive?"

"How should I know?" said Cerys. "You're the

one who wants to play detective. But if motive's what you're interested in, there's only one candidate."

"Who?" said Anwen.

Cerys rolled her eyes. "Who do you think? Queen Flavia, of course. With her brother out of the way, she gets to be in charge."

Tonino looked distraught. "That's impossible," he said. "She'd never do anything like that."

"She's already doing most of the hard work, so why wouldn't she want the throne for herself?" said Cerys. "I'm just stating the obvious."

Anwen hated to admit it, but Cerys had a point—Flavia had the most to gain from Thibault's death, and had stepped into his role with barely a minute's pause. She wrote Flavia's name down, and added the Chamberlain's beneath it. "It's not much of a suspect list," she said. "But it's a start."

"Well, I refuse to believe it," said Tonino. "I've worked for Flavia for almost three years, and she's the nicest, most sensible person I've ever met. You'll *never* find any evidence against her. Now, if you'll excuse me, I'm going to sleep." He stomped over to his bed behind the screen, the ground quaking with every step.

"We really didn't mean to upset you," Anwen called after him. When he didn't answer, she touched her throat and canceled the amplification spell. "Maybe this will all seem better in the morning," she said, without much conviction.

Cerys canceled her own spell before replying. "Maybe. I just hope the beds are comfy. I'm a very fussy sleeper."

They trudged into Fortune Hall together and parted without a word on the landing. Anwen took the room across from Cerys's. It was just as grand, and she threw herself down on the bed, which was so soft it seemed to swallow her. Even so, she missed her old bunk bed at home, close under the barrel roof of Eira's cottage, with its chandelier fashioned from the living roots of the oak tree above and the gentle snores of Eira in the bunk below.

For all their opulence, Fortune Hall and the palace felt dark and strange, full of ticks and creaks that seemed too loud to her tiny human ears.

"Anwen?" Cerys's voice reached her through the bedroom door.

"Yes?"

"Do you really think we'll make it home?"

It was a question that had been lurking, unspoken, in the back of Anwen's mind ever since their arrival. "I hope so," she said.

There was silence for a moment, and she wondered

if Cerys had fallen asleep. Then, almost so quietly that she couldn't hear it, "Me too."

Several hours later, Anwen was pacing around the bedroom, her mind too active to let her rest. She practiced the amplification spell again and again, whispering the incantation under her breath for fear of waking Cerys and Tonino, and trying to tweak it just a little each time until the tingle of magic in her throat felt right.

Outside her window, the lantern cast flickering shapes across the nursery floor, and the painted forest on the walls appeared to shift and twitch. Her imagination conjured terrible creatures lurking just out of sight within the foliage. She shuddered, and was tempted to climb into the safety of the bedclothes when she saw real movement. It was quick and fluid—a blob of shadow flowing along the skirting board at the bottom of the wall. It stopped abruptly, and a pair of dark eyes winked in the candlelight.

Anwen breathed a sigh of relief. It was only a mouse. A giant mouse, of course, almost five feet tall in human measurements, but a house mouse nonetheless.

She opened the bedroom window, leaned out, and

made sure to cancel the amplification spell. "Hey!" she called. "Over here!"

The mouse sat up and sniffed the air, its moonlike ears twitching. Even without the magic in her voice, it could hear her perfectly.

"Here I am," Anwen called, waving. "Can I talk to you?"

The mouse took a few nervous steps in her direction, then paused again as Tonino turned over and murmured in his sleep.

"That's it," said Anwen. "I'd like to ask you some questions."

The mouse watched her intently. Then it bolted, almost too quick to see, toward the corner of the room in which Tonino was sleeping.

"Drat," said Anwen, and turned back to the bed, where her notebook lay open on the covers. She hadn't added anything to her earlier notes except for one big question mark. She still had so many questions to answer, and less than two days before the giants sent her and Cerys home. All she knew for certain was where Thibault had died.

Then, as she stood there fretting, an idea struck her. She hurried to Cerys's bedroom. "Wake up," she said, shaking the Cerys-shaped lump under the covers.

"Whuuuuuh?" said Cerys.

"We need to get back into Thibault's room," said Anwen.

Cerys sat up, bleary-eyed. "Why?"

"To find more clues, of course," said Anwen. "The killer must have left some other trace behind. Maybe it's something too small for the Captain and his guards to notice, but I bet we could find it. We just need to try."

"Anwen, it's the middle of the night," said Cerys.

"The perfect time," she replied. "No one will interrupt us. Come on!" She picked up Cerys's shoes and dangled them over her head.

Cerys snatched them from her and threw them back onto the floor. "Don't be ridiculous. It would take us hours to walk there, and we can't even get out of the nursery. The door's closed, and there's a guard outside."

Anwen grinned. "Leave that to me."

11

Members of Mischief

Anwen dragged a protesting Cerys by the hand across the darkened nursery floor. She couldn't really blame Cerys for being unhappy with her—the nursery was easily the size of Farmer Pebin's apple orchard back home, and it took them several minutes to reach the shadowy corner where Tonino lay sleeping. As they approached it, Anwen saw what she needed—a narrow gap at the foot of the wall, where the two skirting boards met. It was almost invisible unless you looked at it straight on.

"I knew it," she said. "In we go."

Cerys recoiled from the opening. "I'm not going in there."

"It's not dangerous," said Anwen. "Probably."

"Then go in by yourself," said Cerys. "You can tell me all about it in the morning."

"But I need you with me," said Anwen. "It's dark in there, and you're the only one of us who knows how to make a glamour light. Please?"

Cerys put her hands on her hips. "What's in there, anyway?"

"Mice."

Cerys looked horrified. "You want me to crawl into a dark hole full of giant rodents."

"I think they can help us," said Anwen. "Mice are always watching and listening, and I bet they know their way around the palace better than anyone."

"Why don't we just wake Tonino up, and ask him to carry us to Thibault's room?"

"Because he's probably still cross with us for considering Queen Flavia a suspect," Anwen replied. "And he wouldn't be able to get there without passing the guard. Mice can go almost anywhere unseen."

"What if they decide we're food?"

"They're mice, Cerys, not piranhas. I chat with them all the time back home. We'll be fine."

Cerys scowled at the gap in the skirting. "If that's true," she said, "you go in first."

The gap was so low that Anwen had to wriggle through it on her hands and knees. Cerys squirmed through after her, panting and complaining about what the splinters were doing to her new pajamas. At last, they both stood side by side in total darkness.

"Gwawl," said Cerys, and an orb of light about the size of an apple, leapt from her palm. It hovered over them both, illuminating the narrow, dusty space within the wall. Its sides were made of rough brick, crisscrossed with cobwebs that flapped like ghostly bedsheets. The floor was coated with an ankle-deep layer of dust, but, looking around, Anwen saw a clear trail cutting through it, heading away to their left.

"A mouse run," she said, and struck out along the trail. Cerys followed, the light bobbing along above her. Things crawled and skittered across their path—they had to step over a couple of woodlice as big as cats, while a jet-black spider, almost six feet across, crouched in its web overhead and watched them pass with its cluster of eyes.

"Just so you know," whispered Cerys, "I hate everything about this."

Anwen was going to shush her when she heard a rapid patter of feet in the darkness up ahead. The sound drew nearer, then stopped just outside the glow of the light. A pair of dark eyes winked at them.

"What is it?" said Cerys, hugging herself.

"Exactly what we're looking for," said Anwen. "Hello, mouse. Remember me?" She went down on one knee and extended a hand in greeting.

The mouse took a timid hop forward and sniffed her fingers.

"I'm Anwen, this is Cerys, and we'd like your help. Do you speak for the mischief?"

"For the what?" asked Cerys.

"Mischief," said Anwen. "It's what you call a group of mice."

"Oh."

The mouse raised itself up on its hind paws and squeaked loudly. Within seconds, the space behind it was filled with more shining eyes and glinting whiskers. Anwen counted at least eight animals.

"You didn't say there would be this many," said Cerys, her glamour light flickering uncertainly.

"Mischiefs are always fairly big," said Anwen. "These are the scouts. It's their job to search for food and watch for predators."

"As long as *we're* not food," said Cerys.

Anwen rolled her eyes and turned back to the mice. "Hello, everyone," she said. "I know my friend and I look strange, but we wondered if you'd be interested in working together."

The mice pushed forward, pawing and sniffing at them both. The lead mouse, which was gray with a brownish stripe down its side, put himself nose to nose with Anwen and squeaked again.

"Think of it as a swap," said Anwen. "We have lots of food delivered to our room each day. You can probably still smell it on us." She offered her hands for the lead mouse to inspect. It did so, and twitched its whiskers excitedly. "Good, isn't it?" she said. "We'd be happy to save some for you, in return for safe passage through your mouse runs, and a guide, if you can spare someone."

The lead mouse turned to its fellows and a conversation of agitated squeaks ensued.

"I think it's going well," Anwen whispered. "The lead mouse says his name is Garibaldi. He's making our case for us with the others."

"I'm thrilled," said Cerys, who was being given a thorough sniffing by a couple of curious mice. She looked like she wanted to be almost anywhere else.

Anwen put her hand between one of the mouse's ears and stroked its fur. "They like you," she said. "Just give them a bit of attention in return."

The mouse immediately went limp, shut its eyes, and leaned into her touch. Hesitantly, Cerys patted the other mouse on the head. It nuzzled closer to her.

"I suppose they are quite soft," she said, stroking the creature more confidently.

They both turned at a series of squeaks from Garibaldi.

"They've agreed!" said Anwen. "Can you take us to King Thibault's room, please?"

Garibaldi's whiskers twitched, and another exchange of squeaks broke out with the rest of the mischief.

“They don’t know which room I mean,” said Anwen. “I don’t think they can tell one giant from another.”

“Let me handle this,” said Cerys. She made a series of intricate gestures with her hands. As she did so, the glamour light expanded and shifted into the form of a guitar.

“There!” said Anwen, pointing at it. “That’s where we want to go.”

The mischief conferred once more, and Garibaldi rendered their verdict.

“Well?” asked Cerys.

“He says they can take us,” said Anwen. “They just need to make a stop on the way.”

Riding a mouse was not at all like riding a horse, Anwen quickly discovered. They were faster, for one thing—much faster—and their silky fur made holding on extremely difficult.

She lay flat across Garibaldi’s back, her knees gripping his sides as he raced through the narrow confines of the mouse runs. She could hear Cerys wailing with terror somewhere behind her as the rest of the mischief followed close at their heels. They rocketed through wall cavities, jumping rusty nails and old joists, before dropping through holes and sprinting along under floorboards so low that they brushed the back of Anwen's hair. She shut her eyes and prayed that she wouldn't fall.

She had only a vague impression of where they were, but suspected they were following the hallway past Thibault's room, to the other end of the building. This was confirmed when Garibaldi leapt back up through the floorboards into the wall cavity, and skittered to a halt beside a low space that had been dug through the brickwork. Anwen slid off his back and landed on the floor with a thump, her limbs trembling with adrenaline. A second later, the other mice arrived and Cerys landed beside her.

"I'm never doing that again," Cerys panted. Her glamour light had turned a sickly shade of green.

"It's quicker than walking," said Anwen. "It would have taken us ages to get here without them."

Cerys looked around. "Where is *here*, anyway?"

Garibaldi ducked into the gap between the bricks, then reappeared. He squeaked at Anwen.

"He says one of the scouts smelled food," she said. "They're stopping to load up before they take us to Thibault's room."

"They're putting food over a murder investigation?"

"They've got families to feed, Cerys. They're not a passenger service."

"Fine," Cerys replied. "Anything that gives my stomach time to catch up with the rest of me."

They squirmed through the gap after the mice and emerged into the bottom of what looked like a perfectly smooth canyon. One cliff face was the wall of the room, and the other, they soon discovered, was the back of a dresser. They stepped out from behind it into a darkened bedroom—smaller than the nursery, and far more simply decorated than Thibault's quarters. A guest room, Anwen supposed.

The mice swarmed around a plate that was tucked almost out of sight beneath the bed. It was empty, Anwen saw, except for a congealed puddle of grease and an untouched pile of caramelized grapes.

"Yuck," said Cerys. "It looks like it's been sitting here for hours."

"I wonder why the servants haven't cleared it away," said Anwen as the mice tucked in. "The rest of the room is spotless."

In fact, she reflected, the room looked completely untouched. The only item of interest was a leather carryall, the size of an Old Stump cottage, on the floor beside the dresser. A luggage tag tied to one of the handles read UMBERTO.

"How long is this going to take?" asked Cerys, looking nervously from the bag to the door. "What if someone comes back?"

The words had barely left her mouth when the door swung open. The mice reacted instantly, moving as one to the deep shadows under the bed. Cerys snuffed out her glamour light, grabbed Anwen, and pulled her after them.

They all crouched together, silent and motionless, as a pair of booted feet entered the room. A match flared, a lantern was lit, and the boots paced briefly up and down beside the bed before a second pair of feet entered. These were wrapped in silk slippers and almost hidden by the hem of a black dress.

"I know it's the middle of the night, Captain, but I still have a lot of work to do." The voice belonged to Queen Flavia.

"Sorry, Your Majesty, but this couldn't wait," the Captain replied. "When did you last see Professor Umberto?"

There was a startled pause. "He dined with me and Thibault before the concert. Why?"

The Captain began pacing again, with slow, deliberate steps. "You ate together in the banquet hall?"

"Yes," Flavia replied. "But the Professor felt unwell and left the meal early."

"Did he say what was wrong?"

"Travel sickness," she said. "He'd spent all day in the stagecoach from Mountain Fall."

The Captain's boots continued their march. "Have you seen the Professor since he excused himself?"

"No," said Flavia. "He's been recovering in his room, and I had things to attend to. With everything else that's happened since . . ." She tapped the toes of one foot impatiently. "What's all this about?"

The Captain stopped pacing, and Anwen could tell he was standing a little straighter.

"This is the Professor's room, ma'am," he said. "He's not here."

"Then where is he?"

"He doesn't seem to be anywhere," the Captain replied. "He's disappeared."

Anwen grabbed Cerys's hand. Another disappearance!

When Queen Flavia spoke again, she sounded flustered. "What do you mean?"

"The guards confirm that he hasn't left his room all day," said the Captain. "And there's no record of him leaving the palace. But he's not here either."

"Are you sure?" she said. "I arranged for meals to be sent up, and none of them came back."

"There are leftovers here," the Captain replied.

Anwen, Cerys, and the mice shrank back as his hand reached down into view and picked up the plate. "Do you know when this was sent, and who brought it to him?"

"You'd have to ask the kitchen," said Flavia.

"I'll do it first thing in the morning," said the Captain. "And the chambermaids? Who made up the room today?"

"I have absolutely no idea." Flavia's voice sounded strained. "What if he's just exploring the palace?"

"Not without being seen," said the Captain. "And my guards have searched every room in the building. He's gone."

"Meaning what?" said Flavia.

Anwen heard the Captain draw in a slow breath.

"It can't be a coincidence," he said, "that two people have disappeared from their rooms, under armed guard, without anybody noticing."

"You think there's a connection to Thibault's murder," said Flavia.

"I do," the Captain replied. "I just don't know what it is yet. Did your brother and the Professor know each other at all?"

"No, they hadn't met before the banquet," said Flavia. "Professor Umberto was here at my invitation."

"Can I ask why you invited him?" asked the Captain.

"He's a celebrated composer. I wanted to meet him, so I invited him to hear Thibault play."

"How did it go?"

Flavia tutted. "Disastrously. Thibault was horrifically rude, as usual. He refused to engage with the Professor at all."

"How did the Professor react? Was he angry?"

The toes of the silk slipper started tapping the carpet again, but quicker this time. "Captain, if I had any reason to suspect that Professor Umberto posed a danger, I would have notified you immediately. He's quite harmless."

"Of course, Your Majesty," said the Captain. "I just needed to be sure."

Flavia sighed. "I'll be in the throne room if there's any news. And while you're at it, I suggest you have someone send one of the kitchen cats up here. Those leftovers appear to have attracted mice."

She swept out of the room. The Captain lingered for a moment before extinguishing the lamp and following her, pulling the door shut behind him. When his footsteps had faded entirely from their hearing, the mice formed an animated huddle. Garibaldi squeaked rapidly.

"They recognized the word *cat*," said Anwen. "It's not safe for them here anymore."

"Which means it's not safe for us either," said Cerys. "Let's go."

12

Fallen Treasure

A dawn breeze blew across the fallen giant, lifting the ash from the crumbled beanstalk high into the air. Eira stood on her doorstep and watched the gray clouds dissipate toward the Usbrid Woods.

"Good riddance," she muttered. It was one fewer problem to contend with. The people of Old Stump had all been rehoused, albeit temporarily, in neighboring farms and villages, but it had kept her busy into the early hours of the morning. She was tired and anxious—there was still no news of Anwen and Cerys, and she was beginning to imagine the worst. Not even a strong pot of tea had been enough to lift her mood.

"Shall I put the kettle on again?" asked Meredith, emerging from the oak cottage, munching on a slice of toast.

Eira cracked her knuckles and surveyed the surrounding fields. Huge fragments of white marble jutted into the air, like the ruins of some ancient temple. "Maybe later," she said. "There's something I want to go and look for first."

"What's that?" asked Meredith.

"I don't know," said Eira. "I'm hoping I'll know it when I find it."

Five minutes later, the two friends were wandering among the chunks of marble.

"I saw it fall into our world along with all this rubble yesterday," said Eira. "Only for a second, but it was very distinctive. Gold and white, I think, and smaller than all this wreckage. It came down somewhere in this part of the field."

"Are you sure?" asked Meredith.

"No," said Eira. "There was a lot going on."

They continued their search in silence for a few minutes, kicking over smaller fragments of stone.

"Where's Stillpike this morning?" asked Eira.

"He got back from delivering your message to Oldport in the middle of the night," said Meredith. "He's probably camped under a tree somewhere, getting some sleep."

Eira nodded. Stillpike moved from place to place as work demanded, pitching a tattered one-man tent wherever he fancied. "Perhaps we should go and fetch him," she said. "We could use the help."

"No need," said Meredith.

"Why not?"

"Because I think I've just found what you're after."

She rolled a fragment of marble aside and pointed at something half buried in the soil. Something gold.

"Meredith, you must still have some of my luck potion on you," said Eira. "That looks like exactly the thing."

It took them a few minutes to dig away the earth around the object, but Eira had a pretty clear idea of what it was before they were even half-finished—it was a piece of giant jewelry in the form of a musical clef, made from gold, with white-gold highlights. It was about twenty inches across, and very heavy. She and Meredith were both panting when they finally hauled it clear of the earth.

"Is it a brooch?" asked Meredith.

"A cuff link," Eira replied, examining the T-shaped fastening on the back. "For pinning shirt cuffs together."

"From our dead giant, d'you think?"

"Possibly," said Eira. "I'll have to check his sleeves to be sure."

"What shall we do with it in the meantime?"

Eira wiped the sweat from her forehead. "Help me get it to the cottage. We can't leave it here; it might be evidence."

"Evidence of what?"

"There's been a murder," said Eira. "Every little detail could count in solving it." She tightened her grip on the cuff link and, together, she and Meredith began staggering back toward the cottage.

"That's not our job, is it?" asked Meredith, her cheeks red with effort.

"To look after the crime scene?" said Eira. "Yes. I just hope there's someone up there in the Sky Kingdom taking care of everything else." *And taking care of you, Anwen*, she thought.

13

Intrigue for Breakfast

By the time Anwen awoke, the nursery was flooded with sunlight, which streamed in through the windows of Fortune Hall. "Cerys?" she called.

"Downstairs" came the reply.

Anwen found her in the kitchen, wearing a red evening gown with silver trim. "Dressing for breakfast?" she asked, taking a seat across the table.

"If breakfast ever gets here," said Cerys. "I'm starving, and all this food is porcelain." She tapped a bowl of ceramic fruit with her knuckles.

Anwen's stomach growled in sympathy. "Let's ask Tonino for something."

"He's not here," Cerys replied. "He was gone when I woke up. He must still be cross with us."

A tingle of disquiet ran down Anwen's spine as she remembered Professor Umberto's empty guest bedroom. What if Tonino had disappeared as well?

Her thoughts were interrupted by a knock at the nursery door.

"Hello?" came a woman's voice. "Can I come in?"

Before Cerys could reply, Anwen touched her

hand to her throat, spoke the incantation, and, with a perfectly amplified voice, called, "Yes, go ahead."

Cerys blinked in surprise. "When did you figure that out?"

Anwen couldn't help looking a bit smug as she led the way out of the kitchen, out of Fortune Hall's front door, and onto the nursery floor.

A round, late-middle-aged woman with a bun of gray hair stepped into the room. She wore a maid's uniform.

"Gabriela!" exclaimed Anwen.

Gabriela stopped short, looked around and then down. "That's right," she said. "How ever did you know?"

Anwen remembered, too late, that Gabriela had no idea she had been present in Thibault's chambers the previous evening. "Oh, um, Tonino told us all about you," she said. "He was worried, after what happened last night."

"Bless him," said Gabriela. "He's a good boy."

"Do you know where he is?" asked Cerys, applying her own amplification spell.

"In the throne room, on some business for Her Majesty," said Gabriela. "I'm here to make your beds and check the place is nice and tidy for you." She approached them with a mixture of caution and fascination. "Why, you really are the most perfect little things I've ever seen," she said. "I can hardly believe you're real."

"Thank you," said Cerys. "I'm Cerys Powell, Grand High Witch of the Land Below, and this is Anwen, my humble assistant."

"Ignore her," said Anwen. "It's very nice to meet you, Gabriela."

"Likewise, I'm sure. Now let's get your rooms sorted, shall we?" Gabriela reached over them and opened up the front of the dollhouse. "Dear oh dear," she said, eyeing the piles of clothes scattered around Cerys's bedroom. "Almost as bad as His Majesty, may he rest in peace."

The girls stood aside as Gabriela knelt down and began replacing the clothes on their hangers, which were so small that she had to pinch them between finger and thumb. Anwen remembered what Tonino had told her about Gabriela having to clean up after Thibault every day.

"Was King Thibault very messy as well?" she asked.

Gabriela cast a guilty look over her shoulder. "I shouldn't speak ill of the dead," she said. "But he was messy as a teenager, and I've raised two of them, so I should know. I blame that guitar of his."

“The guitar?” said Anwen. “Why?”

“It was his obsession,” Gabriela replied. “He spent hours locked in his chambers every day, practicing, while his poor sister filled in for him. He wouldn’t even let me into the room with it unless he was there to keep an eye on me.”

“He sounds a bit paranoid,” said Cerys.

Gabriela hung the dresses back in the wardrobes and shut the doors with her fingertips. “He was probably worried about the Maestro,” she said.

Anwen wished she could pull her notebook out and start scribbling all this down. “Who?”

“The Maestro,” said Gabriela. “He’s a fancy classical musician over at the Royal School of the Arts. Old King Augustus—that’s Thibault and Flavia’s father—hired him as their music tutor when they were younger, but it didn’t work out. At least, not for Thibault.”

“What happened?” asked Anwen.

“Thibault just didn’t have the knack for music,” said Gabriela. “He tried almost everything—viola, harpsichord, flute . . . But after ten years of lessons, he still couldn’t carry a tune in a bucket. He was so bad, the Maestro gave up in disgust.”

Anwen raised her eyebrows. “Then who taught him to play the guitar?”

"That's the odd thing," said Gabriela. "He taught himself, or so he said. He found the guitar stashed in the palace attic a few years ago, picked it up, and everything clicked. Within a few weeks he was performing for the public. It took us all by surprise."

Anwen's brain itched as it digested all this new information. "What would the Maestro want with Thibault's guitar?" she asked.

"They had a big falling out," said Gabriela. She lifted Cerys's four-poster bed out of the dollhouse with one hand and stripped the bedclothes from it. The sheets looked no bigger than handkerchiefs in her grasp. "The Maestro was furious that Thibault had turned himself into a musical star overnight, when the Maestro hadn't been able to teach him a single note. And playing a commoner's instrument, no less! He wrote letters to the newspapers, calling Thibault a fraud. He said the guitar must be enchanted."

"But giants can't use magic, can they?" said Cerys.

"Quite," said Gabriela. "Nobody took him seriously, but it was enough to get him a lifetime ban from the palace." She pulled new doll-sized bedsheets from a pocket in her apron and applied them to the bed, expertly folding down the corners. This job done, she replaced the bed in Cerys's room and moved on to Anwen's. It was amazing to watch such heavy furniture being handled like toys. *Which they technically are*, Anwen thought.

"Do you think the Maestro killed Thibault?" she asked.

Gabriela paused. "His Majesty could be difficult, goodness knows," she said. "But I don't think their disagreement was that bad, and the Maestro hasn't set foot inside the palace for months."

Except the killer was able to sneak in and out of Thibault's room as if they were invisible, thought Anwen. *So how sure can we be?*

Gabriela was replacing Anwen's bed when Tonino arrived.

"Sorry I'm late," he said. "Her Majesty needed me for something, but I made sure to bring you both extra breakfast." He proffered a small saucer, piled high with miniature sugared pastries, each the size of his little finger. "Truce?" he said.

"Truce!" said Cerys, staring wide-eyed at the plate.

Tonino looked relieved. "Morning, Gabriela. How are you feeling today?"

"Much better for some sleep. Thanks, love. Just let me deal with the other dollhouse and I'll be out of your hair." She looked around the room. "Where is it?"

"Fame Hall?" said Tonino. "Someone must have moved it. We don't know where it's gone."

"Oh well, that saves me a job." She bundled Anwen's and Cerys's bedclothes into a ball in one hand. "I'll send these straight down to the laundry room."

She crossed to the rear wall and pressed a knot in the bark of one of the trees in the mural. Anwen had assumed it was just a painting like all the others, but, with a soft click, a section of the wall swung open, revealing a dark recess, about fifty feet across. Gabriela tossed the bedclothes in, and was swinging the panel shut when Anwen spoke up.

"Wait! What's that?"

"This?" said Gabriela. "Just a laundry chute."

Anwen's curiosity was piqued. "May I see it?"

"It's nothing terribly exciting," said Gabriela. Nevertheless, she stooped down and extended her hand, and Anwen practically ran onto it. Moving cautiously, Gabriela carried her to the open panel. "Mind you hold on tight now," she said. "It's a long way down."

The chute was like a great metal chimney, wide enough to swallow any of the cottages in Old Stump. Anwen peered nervously over the edge of Gabriela's hand, into thousands of feet of darkness.

"Where does it lead?" she asked.

"To the laundry room in the basement," said Gabriela.

Anwen felt a new piece of the puzzle taking shape in her imagination. "Do all the bedrooms in the palace have laundry chutes?"

"Most of them," Gabriela replied. "We chambermaids can't spend all our time staggering up and down stairs with dirty linen, you know."

"Including Thibault's room?" asked Anwen.

"Of course," said Gabriela.

Anwen thrilled as the new puzzle piece clicked into place, and she realized it intersected with something she had overheard Gabriela say in Thibault's chambers the night before.

"Wait. Did you change Thibault's bedclothes too?"

"Every morning," Gabriela replied. "Once I'd persuaded him to drag himself out of the old ones."

"What about yesterday morning?" asked Anwen. "The morning he was missing. Tonino mentioned you found something different."

"Did I?" said Tonino. Anwen shot him a meaningful look. "I mean, I did," he said.

"It was nothing really," said Gabriela. "But when I went into his room, it wasn't just him that was missing—he'd stripped all his bedclothes, and I couldn't find them anywhere. He must have put them down the chute himself."

"Is that unusual?" asked Anwen.

"I suppose so, but I was too busy to think about it, so I just put new sheets down and got on with things." She looked thoughtful. "Do you think it's important?"

All of Anwen's instincts were screaming the answer at her. "Yes," she said. "I think it's how the murderer got into and out of Thibault's room without passing the guards. Did you tell Captain Adami about it?"

Gabriela shook her head.

"Tell me about what?"

The Captain had appeared in the open doorway. There were deep bags under his eyes, and Anwen guessed he hadn't slept at all last night, but he listened attentively as Gabriela put Anwen back on the floor and told him about the missing bedsheets.

"Thank you, Gabby," he said. "I'll look into it."

She bobbed a curtsy, made her goodbyes, and slipped out.

The Captain crossed to the laundry chute and swung the hatch shut. "If I didn't know any better, I'd say that you two were conducting your own investigation," he said. "Should I be keeping a closer eye on you?"

Cerys jabbed a finger at Anwen. "It's her idea!"

"I was just asking questions," said Anwen.

The hint of a smile played at the edge of the Captain's lips. "At least they're good ones," he said.

"And for what it's worth, I agree that the killer probably escaped from Thibault's room down the laundry chute. But they couldn't have gotten in that way."

"Why not?" asked Anwen.

"There's a one-way, spring-loaded trapdoor built into each chute. It drops open when laundry lands on it from above, then it automatically closes again. And it can't be opened from underneath. It's a security measure."

Anwen's excitement turned into frustration. She had been so certain she'd solved both parts of the problem. "That's quite clever," she said grudgingly.

"We're not complete amateurs," said the Captain. "And I'll ask you again to leave this investigation to the professionals."

Anwen felt like a child who had just been dismissed by an impatient parent. She hated it, but nodded.

"Thank you," said the Captain. "Now, I need to ask Tonino a few questions while you finish your breakfast."

Tonino reached into Fortune Hall, cleared the kitchen table, and set the saucer down on it. The pastries, which had looked small in his hands, were each the size of a loaf of human bread, and each cake could have fed a family of four.

Anwen and Cerys hurried to the kitchen and

each seized an oversized croissant dusted with powdered sugar. Anwen took a bite and discovered, to her delight, that it was stuffed with a sweet cinnamon cream that melted on her tongue. She wondered if the rulers in her own world had ever eaten so well.

"Am I in trouble, sir?" Tonino asked.

"Nothing like that," said the Captain. "I was just wondering what you can tell me about Professor Umberto."

Anwen almost sprayed a blizzard of pastry flakes all over herself. She exchanged a look with Cerys, and snuck her notebook from her pocket under the table.

Cerys broke the amplification spell on her voice. "What are you doing?" she asked. "You just told him you weren't going to investigate anymore."

Anwen broke her own amplification spell. "Maybe I'm just keeping a journal," she replied. "That's not against the rules."

Tonino straightened his waistcoat. "The composer Her Majesty invited to the concert?" he said. "I saw him briefly at the banquet before he was taken ill."

"What about yesterday?" asked the Captain.

"No, sir."

"Really?" said the Captain. "Because I checked with the kitchen staff and they told me Her Majesty assigned you to bring him his meals."

Tonino swallowed loudly. "He didn't want to be disturbed, so I left them outside his door."

"You spoke to him?"

Tonino nodded as if his head might fall off.

"But you didn't see him."

"No, sir. We spoke through the door. I think he was still ill."

"But not too ill to eat," said the Captain. He watched Tonino closely, like a hawk eyeing a rabbit. Beads of sweat started to form on the page boy's forehead.

"Who cleaned his room yesterday?" asked the Captain.

"I don't know, sir," said Tonino. "One of the chambermaids?"

"None of the chambermaids," said the Captain. "They had orders from the queen not to disturb him. Did you do it?"

"No, sir." Tonino wiped the sweat from his forehead with his sleeve. "Is the Professor all right?"

The Captain pulled his own notebook from his pocket and began taking the details down. "I'll tell you when I find him."

Anwen turned to Cerys excitedly. "I knew there was something strange about that guest room," she said. "It was too clean, as if nobody had stayed there at all."

Cerys shook her head. "Someone must have been there," she replied. "Otherwise, who was Tonino taking the meals to? We saw the leftovers."

It was yet another question that Anwen couldn't answer, and it gnawed uncomfortably at her thoughts. "If Professor Umberto *was* in there, what happened to him?"

"Maybe he was kidnapped," Cerys replied.

"But there were no signs of a struggle," said Anwen. "And why didn't anyone see him leave?"

Cerys threw her hands up. "I don't know! I just want to finish breakfast." She picked up her croissant and took an enormous mouthful.

Anwen's croissant sat forgotten. "Maybe someone tidied the room after the Professor disappeared," she said to herself. "But why do such a thorough job and leave the plate of leftovers behind? Unless the Professor wasn't in there to begin with. But that would mean . . ." She raised her eyes to Tonino, who was nervously watching the Captain finish his notes. *That would mean that Tonino just lied*, she thought. *But he wouldn't do that, would he?*

The idea was so unnerving that she shoved it to the very back of her mind. *Of course not*, she reasoned. *Tonino's nice. He's helping us.*

"Thank you, Tonino," said the Captain, closing

the book. "I might have more questions for you later." He doffed his helmet in the girls' direction, and made for the door.

Anwen waved goodbye to him and turned back to Cerys. "We need to take another look at Thibault's room as soon as possible," she said. "If the Professor's involved in his murder, we might find some clues."

But Cerys didn't reply. She was staring in terror at the nursery door, the croissant halfway to her lips. A dollop of cream slid out of it and splattered onto her dress.

Anwen turned, and went rigid. The Captain was stepping outside, but something had slipped into the room between his feet—a sleek gray cat. Its emerald eyes were fixed unwaveringly on them.

"Oh no," said Anwen. "It must smell mouse on us." She had never had a reason to be afraid of cats before, but then she'd never encountered one three times her height. "There's no need to panic," she said as the creature tensed, ready to pounce. "Let me see if I can talk to it, and—"

"Help!" yelled Cerys, springing back from the table. The cat surged forward, teeth bared.

Tonino and the Captain leapt for it, but it was too fast for them—the beast sprang, claws reaching for the open front of Fortune Hall. Cerys screamed, and Anwen jumped to her feet.

"Stop!" she shouted. But as the cat's shadow fell over her, she knew that it was hopeless. She was about to become breakfast.

14

Reminiscences

The monstrous cat lunged through the open front of Fortune Hall's kitchen, its eyes blazing, its breath like an oven full of old meat. Anwen braced herself for the tearing pain of its teeth, but the animal batted her aside with its paw, and she sprawled across the kitchen table, winded.

Why hadn't it killed her? Then she saw Cerys with her back pressed against the sink. Maybe it was the screaming, or the bright fabric of her dress, but the cat wanted her more. It reached for her, ready to hook her into its mouth.

"Don't!" shouted Anwen. "She tastes terrible! Eat me instead!"

The beast's enormous head swung around and fixed her with its emerald gaze. It seemed surprised to be spoken to by its next meal, but Anwen knew cats well enough to realize that its hesitation wouldn't last. She rolled off the table a second before the cat knocked it flying, scattering breakfast everywhere.

She landed on her back, completely exposed. The cat purred with anticipation as it leaned over her and opened its jaws . . .

They snapped shut a few inches in front of her face. The cat's eyes widened, and it disappeared backward out of the kitchen with a yowl of protest. Anwen saw Tonino's hand gripping it by the tail before the Captain's anxious face filled her view out into the nursery.

"Are you both all right?" he said.

Anwen pushed herself onto her elbows and activated her amplification spell. "I think so."

"That thing almost *ate* us!" said Cerys, having also amplified her voice. She was pale and shaking, but unharmed.

The Captain breathed a sigh of relief. "I'm sorry," he said. "It was supposed to be hunting mice in one of the guest rooms. I don't know what brought it in here."

Anwen hoped that her look of guilt was too small for him to notice, although she couldn't hide it from Cerys, who glared at her.

The crockery rattled as the Captain jumped to his feet. "Tonino, take that animal back down to the kitchens, and make sure nobody lets any more cats out while the ambassadors are with us. I don't care how many mice we've got."

Anwen ventured onto the nursery carpet in time to see Tonino hurry out of the room, clutching the clawing, spitting ball of gray fur to his chest. The cat looked daggers at her across the room, and then was gone.

The Captain removed his helmet and dragged his hand across his face. "This is my fault," he said, sitting heavily on the toy chest. "I should have been more alert."

"Don't be too hard on yourself," said Anwen. "Cats go where they want, and they never follow orders. Not even from captains."

"That's very kind," he said. "But if anything had happened to either of you . . ." He shook his head. "There's been too much death on my watch already."

"I normally never admit this, but Anwen's right," said Cerys, stepping out of Fortune Hall. "This wasn't your fault. Although . . ." She turned to Anwen. "I'm sure I do *not* taste terrible. In fact, I'm probably delicious."

"I had to say something to get its attention," said Anwen. "And I didn't have time for the formalities."

"What formalities?" asked Cerys.

"It's a cat thing," Anwen replied. "They all claim they're descended from ancient gods, and expect to be treated like it. It's nonsense, of course, but there's no arguing with a cat. Like I said, they don't follow orders, but they will follow food."

Cerys looked at her feet. "Yes. Well. Thanks for making sure that food wasn't me."

With a start, Anwen realized that Cerys had never thanked her for anything before. "You're welcome," she replied.

There was a rasping sound, like a thousand sheets of sandpaper being dragged across a tree trunk, and she looked up to see the Captain stroking the stubble on his chin. "You can speak to animals?" he asked.

"It's a Meadow Witch necessity," Anwen replied. "Our magic is tied to nature, and nobody knows nature like animals. It's just polite to get their perspective."

"Incredible," said the Captain. "Do they all speak their own languages? Do you have to learn to moo, if you're talking to a cow?"

Cerys tittered, and Anwen gave her a withering look. "Animals all think and communicate differently, but my grandma taught me a charm of comprehension when I was very young. It's pretty basic—hardly even a proper spell at all, really—but it helps to make their meanings clear, and helps them understand me in return."

"How about a charm for sorting truth from lies?" asked the Captain.

"No, sorry."

He gave a tired smile. "Looks like I'm stuck with good old-fashioned legwork," he said. "I'll get back to it as soon as Tonino returns to look after you."

The mention of Tonino made Anwen's doubts resurface. Could he really know more about Professor Umberto's disappearance than he claimed? The idea made her stomach knot, and she tensed as the nursery door opened, but it was only Marcus.

"Cato," he said. "Got a minute?"

"Barely," said the Captain. "What's wrong?"

"With me? Nothing. It's you I'm worried about."

He greeted Anwen and Cerys with a tug of his forelock. "I hope he's not giving you two a hard time. He's always cranky before breakfast."

"No, I'm not," said the Captain.

"I know how he feels," said Cerys, surveying the pastries that lay scattered over the floor.

Marcus dragged a rocking horse over to the toy chest and sat astride it, facing the Captain. "You look tired," he said. "Did you pull an all-nighter?"

The Captain bristled. "There's a killer on the loose."

"And you'll never catch them if you're exhausted," said Marcus. "You should get some rest."

"Later, maybe."

Marcus turned in exasperation to Anwen and

Cerys. "Can you two persuade him? He never listened to me, even when we were kids."

"I didn't realize you've known each other that long," said Anwen.

"We grew up together," said the Captain. "The Taliedo Street orphanage. It was the roughest dive in town, so we stuck together for protection."

"Did it work?" asked Cerys.

The Captain chuckled. "Not often. That's why we spent most of our time out on the streets, trying to keep out of trouble."

Anwen picked up one of the kitchen chairs, which been hurled out onto the carpet by the cat, and sat down on it. "I can't believe you were both street kids," she said.

"Please," said Marcus. "We prefer to be called urchins." Both men laughed.

"Is that why the Chamberlain was such a snob to you outside the throne room yesterday?" asked Anwen.

"The Chamberlain thinks he's more regal than the actual royals," said Marcus. "But yes, we're definitely the 'wrong sort.'"

Cerys leaned on the back of Anwen's chair. "Then how did you end up here?" she asked.

"Pure chance," said the Captain. "We were supposed to be musicians."

"Not just musicians," said Marcus. "A superstar duo."

The Captain blushed a little. "It sounds silly now, but we thought music was our ticket to the big time. I played a tin flute, and Marcus here had an old guitar someone had thrown out. We used to busk on street corners for coins."

"We got pretty good," said Marcus.

"Not *that* good," the Captain replied.

"So what happened?" asked Anwen.

The two men locked eyes for a moment, and she thought she saw a momentary sadness pass between them.

"You can't be a serious musician in this town unless you've trained at the Royal School of the Arts," said Marcus. "We auditioned for scholarships, but they wouldn't take us."

"Why not?" asked Cerys.

"Because we weren't very good," said the Captain.

"Says you," Marcus replied. "We had real energy."

"But no real talent," said the Captain. "Besides, if they hadn't turned us away, I never would have joined the royal guards."

"I still say you gave up too easily," said Marcus.

"Do you still play?" asked Anwen.

"Whenever I can," Marcus replied. "I got a bit

fired up by Thibault's concert, so as soon as it was over, I broke out my guitar and held my own in the palace kitchens. It might have gotten a bit rowdy."

"Twenty separate complaints about the noise, before I arrived to break it up," added the Captain.

"You should have grabbed your flute and joined in," said Cerys.

The Captain laughed. "I was too busy hunting for the Chamberlain. He'd pulled another one of his vanishing acts."

This made Anwen sit up straighter. *The Chamberlain was missing after Thibault's concert? That was when the murder took place!* She desperately wanted to ask the Captain about it, but knew that he would tell her to drop the matter. Nevertheless, she made a mental note: *The Chamberlain has no alibi!*

Her thoughts were interrupted by Marcus, who dismounted the rocking horse. "Speaking of the Chamberlain, I'd better get back to work before he misses me." He clapped the Captain on the shoulder. "Get some sleep, okay?"

"I'll try," said the Captain. "Thanks, mate."

Marcus left, almost colliding with Tonino, who burst into the room. He sported claw marks on his cheek, and the front of his waistcoat had been shredded.

"Are they really both all right?" he asked. He saw

Anwen and Cerys, and sagged with relief. "Thank goodness."

The Captain got to his feet. "Thanks for the chat, you two. It's just what I needed."

As soon as he was gone, Tonino threw himself down in front of Fortune Hall. The impact felt like an earthquake and almost tipped Anwen off her chair.

"Wow!" he said. "I can't believe a cat got in here. You must have been terrified!"

"It looks like you got the worst of it," Anwen replied. "Thanks for grabbing it when you did."

"No problem," he said. He reached over them and returned the scattered pastries to the plate. "Sorry about breakfast."

"How about brunch?" asked Cerys.

"I'll ask the kitchen to send something up," said Tonino. "But first, Queen Flavia has a job for you."

Anwen and Cerys exchanged a look of surprise.

"What sort of job?" asked Cerys.

"She's sending a letter through the thin place to the Land Below, to warn them we'll be retrieving Thibault's body. She wants you to add a note to your families, so they know you're safe."

"Good idea," said Anwen. "When do you think they're going to finish clearing the rubble?"

"Later today," he replied. "They'll bring the body up at dawn tomorrow."

Cerys applauded. "Then I can finally go to the Academy. I hate to think how much I'll have missed."

Anwen rolled her eyes. "You'll only be a couple of days late," she said. "Stop complaining."

"That's easy for you to say," Cerys replied. "You're not going to miss anything."

Anwen's temper flared. "I miss my grandma," she replied. "And all my neighbors. What about your parents? Don't you miss them?"

"Of course," said Cerys. "But they've given up so much for me to go to the Academy, I won't let them down now."

"Given up what, exactly?" said Anwen.

Cerys looked at her flatly. "For a detective, you're really not much good at seeing what's right in front of you."

Her answer took Anwen aback. "What's that supposed to mean?" Cerys merely folded her arms and put her nose in the air. "Fine," Anwen retorted. "Be like that."

Tonino looked from one to the other in awkward silence. "I'll fetch some writing paper, shall I?" he said.

Half an hour and several abandoned drafts later, Anwen had finally written a note from her and Cerys at the foot of a sheet of paper the size of a ship's sail. Tonino folded it up and was tucking it inside his waistcoat when the sound of splintering stone reached them from outside the palace.

He scooped them up in his hands, opened the window, and leaned his elbows on the casement, scaring away a pigeon that had been sitting on the sill.

A crowd of mourners still thronged the palace gates, and the offerings had grown into an enormous pile. Beyond them, in the piazza, workmen were clearing the ruined monument, breaking up the larger chunks of marble with pickaxes and loading them onto a waiting fleet of carts.

"I told you it wouldn't take long," said Tonino.

Watching the excavation work, Anwen felt as if some of the rubble was clearing from her own mind, and it wasn't long before she uncovered a startling fact.

"I'm an idiot!" she exclaimed.

"Obviously," said Cerys. "But why?"

"I can't believe I didn't think of it before. We've been trying to figure out who could have snuck into Thibault's room after the concert, and how they did it, but we've missed something really obvious."

"What's that?" asked Tonino.

"We know *exactly* where the killer was at noon yesterday. Out there." She pointed at the rubble.

"That's when they dumped Thibault's body through the thin place into our world."

They stood in silence for a moment, and watched the workmen loading the carts.

"How does that help us?" said Cerys. "It's too late to search the rubble for clues."

"Maybe we don't have to," said Anwen. "The killer couldn't have dragged a dead king into the middle of a public square, in broad daylight, without somebody seeing something. We need to find some witnesses."

Tonino cleared his throat. "I might be able to help with that," he said.

Anwen looked up at him, although this mostly gave her a view up his nostrils. "Who should we talk to first?"

"Me," he replied. "I was out there at noon yesterday. And it's not as simple as you think."

15
Monumental Questions

Anwen looked from Tonino to the ruined monument in the piazza below and back again.

"You were out there at the same time as the killer?" she said.

"Not just me," he replied. "The Chamberlain ordered a load of servants to help clean up the piazza the morning after the concert. There were dozens of us."

"Here we go again," said Cerys as Anwen elbowed her aside, pulled out her notebook, and sat cross-legged in the bowl of Tonino's cupped hands. "I'm never going to get brunch, am I?"

"Start with the monument," said Anwen. "Did you see anyone near it?"

"We were all there," Tonino replied. "The staff were split into two teams, you see. One team went out across the piazza with some old laundry bags, picking up litter. When our bags were full, we left them in front of the monument for the second team to take back to the palace."

Anwen reflected on this for a moment, and connected it with what Gabriela had told them earlier.

Laundry bags . . . laundry chutes . . . "How big were these bags?" she asked.

"A few feet across and almost as tall as me."

"Big enough to hide a body in, you mean."

He looked at her in horror. "That's terrible!"

Anwen scribbled the facts down in her notebook. "If the killer dropped Thibault's body down the chute into the laundry room after the concert, they could have hidden it in one of the bags overnight, and then taken it out to the piazza the next morning, during the cleanup. It would be the only way to move it undetected, especially with so many people around. Did anyone stay at the monument the whole time?"

"Only the Chamberlain. He was directing everyone."

Cerys looked triumphant. "Ha! I told you he was behind this."

The hairs on Anwen's arms stood up. Could it really be the Chamberlain? He was suffering from headaches, possibly due to a blow to the head from the same bust that killed Thibault. The Captain said he'd gone missing after the concert, and now Tonino had placed him at the scene when Thibault's body had been dumped.

But in the midst of her excitement, her grandmother's voice spoke up from her subconscious: *Are you looking for the easy answer, or the* right *answer?*

It was a question that made her stop and think again. Why would the Chamberlain want Thibault dead? Even with all the evidence mounting up, none of it made sense without a motive. She brooded over the question as Cerys spoke up.

"Whoever the killer is, how did they reach the thin place if there was a huge statue built on top of it?"

"Good point," said Anwen. "What exactly did the monument look like?"

Tonino thought for a moment, then placed Anwen and Cerys carefully down on the carpet. "I think there's a drawing of it hanging in one of the hallways," he said. "Hang on." He bolted from the room, but was back within a minute, carrying a framed etching almost as tall as he was. "Here it is," he said, leaning it against the wall.

It depicted a larger-than-life-sized statue of a giant in classical robes, holding a flaming torch aloft, and trampling a stone beanstalk beneath his feet. The whole thing stood on a wide stone plinth.

"We had to learn all about it in history lessons when I was still at school," said Tonino. "It was built after the war, to celebrate the new era of peace, and to seal up the thin place. It's dangerous to have a big hole in the world right in the middle of the city."

Anwen pointed at the torch in the statue's hand. "What's that? The flame doesn't look like a carving."

"The Flame of Eternal Hope," said Tonino. "It burned all day and night, to light the way into a brighter future." He recited the words mechanically, and Anwen guessed he'd been forced to learn them by heart at school.

"Eternal?" she said. "You mean it never went out?"

"That's right."

"Easy," said Cerys. She opened her hand, palm upward, and a bright orange flame blossomed above it.

"Stop showing off," said Anwen. "The statue's flame couldn't have used magic. It must have been real."

"It was," said Tonino. "I saw a pigeon fly into it once. You could smell roast bird from the other side of the piazza." He wrinkled his nose at the memory.

"The only way to keep a real flame burning for that long is to use some sort of fuel," said Anwen. "So it must have had tanks, or a pipeline to feed it." She thought back to the moment when the beanstalk had smashed up through the piazza, and remembered the whiff of gas she'd smelled. "Was there anything under the statue apart from the thin place?"

Tonino's brow creased. "I think so. They taught us there was some sort of mechanism under the monument to keep the flame lit. There was a little door in the back of the plinth, but it was always locked."

"A service room," said Anwen. "Of course. Its

floor must have been right above the thin place. The killer probably just had to dig through it, or pull up some floorboards, to drop Thibault's body through."

"The Chamberlain could totally have done that," said Cerys.

Tonino put his head to one side. "I was busy, so he could have slipped away without me noticing. But he was there when Captain Adami came out to announce that King Thibault was missing."

Anwen looked up sharply. "What time was this?"

"Just after midday," said Tonino. "The Chamberlain ordered us all back inside to join the search parties."

Anwen sucked thoughtfully on the end of her charcoal, leaving a black smudge in the corner of her mouth. "What did his sleeves look like?"

Tonino looked confused. "The same as always, I think. Why?"

"No reason," she replied. She added a final note to her book and slipped it back into her pocket. "Thanks, Tonino."

He beamed at her. "Happy to help. Now, I'd better deliver your letter to Her Majesty."

"Don't forget to bring some food back with you!" said Cerys as he left.

"I have no idea how you can eat so much," said Anwen.

"It's easy when you're always hungry," Cerys replied. As if in confirmation, her stomach growled.

"You're not going to starve before lunchtime," said Anwen. "But we should put some of our breakfast in the mousehole for the mischief to collect."

Cerys looked sadly at the scattered pastries. "What a waste," she said. "The mice didn't even take us where we asked to go."

"They still helped," said Anwen. "Without them, we never would have learned the truth about Professor Umberto."

"I suppose so," said Cerys. "But what about Thibault's room? Do you still want to look for more clues?"

"Absolutely." Anwen paused and scratched her head. "But before we do, perhaps we should figure out which pieces of the puzzle are still missing. Come on." She struck off across the carpet, through the open front of Fortune Hall, and into the wood-paneled drawing room.

"What are we doing here?" asked Cerys, following her.

"This feels like a good thinking room," Anwen replied. She sank into a leather armchair beside the hearth, which was filled with crepe-paper flames.

"Urgh, boring!" said Cerys. "What am I supposed to do while you've got your nose in your notebook?"

"You could help me," Anwen replied.

"I'd rather redecorate," said Cerys. She snapped her fingers, and the dark brown of the wood panels turned bright pink. "The Chamberlain did it. Now go and tell the Captain, so he can arrest him."

"We can't take an accusation to the Captain without proof," said Anwen. "And that pink is horrid."

Cerys snapped her fingers again, and the panels turned to royal blue. "How much more proof do you need?"

"A motive, at least," said Anwen.

"Easy. Queen Flavia ordered him to do it."

Anwen pulled out her notebook again and flipped back through the pages. It was possible, she reflected—Flavia, frustrated with Thibault's laziness, asked one of her most loyal servants to do away with him, so she could take the throne herself.

"We'll need even more proof if we're going to accuse the queen of conspiracy," she said. "And there's one other thing."

"What?" asked Cerys.

"The Chamberlain's sleeves," Anwen replied. "If he'd dug up the floor under the monument, don't you think they would be messy? Tonino didn't spot anything unusual about them at all."

Cerys pouted. "Maybe he was very careful." She

muttered a quick spell, and the burgundy carpet underfoot took on the appearance of sparkling white sand.

"No one can dig a hole *that* carefully," said Anwen, trying to ignore the distraction. "And it doesn't explain why he'd go to all the trouble of dropping Thibault through the thin place to begin with. We know that the killer wasn't trying to cover up the crime, because they left the murder weapon behind."

Cerys settled into an identical armchair facing Anwen's, and turned a nearby table into a large toadstool. "So why do you think they did it?"

"I wish I knew," said Anwen. "But it has to be important, otherwise why bother? Dropping a giant into the human world is a big deal. Big enough to provoke another war, maybe, and that doesn't seem like the sort of thing that Queen Flavia would want." She twisted a strand of her hair around her fingers. "And what's Professor Umberto got to do with all this? His disappearance *has* to be linked to Thibault somehow."

Cerys gazed thoughtfully into the hearth. "Flavia said that the Professor was her favorite composer, so she probably didn't have him killed."

"Agreed," said Anwen.

"And you don't think he was kidnapped, so he must have snuck out of the palace by himself."

"As far as I can tell."

Cerys blinked, and the crepe-paper flames sprang to life. They even glowed and crackled, although they gave off no heat.

"He was probably running from something," said Cerys. "So maybe he *did* kill Thibault. But if that's true, why did he spend the next day sitting in his room?"

With a sinking feeling, Anwen realized she couldn't avoid her doubts any longer. "What if the Professor wasn't in his room that day at all?" she said. "What if Tonino lied to the Captain?"

Cerys sat up straight, her illusions winked out, and the room was back to normal again. "Are you serious?"

Anwen nodded. "You saw the room—it was spotless. If the maids weren't allowed in to tidy it . . ."

"Then it means no one had used it at all," Cerys finished for her.

"It's the only answer that makes sense," said Anwen. "But it means Tonino couldn't have had those conversations with the Professor through the door. The Professor might have disappeared hours earlier than we realized."

"But what about the leftovers?" asked Cerys. "And the overnight bag?"

"Anyone could have put the bag there," said Anwen. "And I suppose Tonino must have let himself into the room and eaten the meals himself."

Cerys looked as devastated as Anwen felt. "I can't believe we trusted him!"

"I don't think he means us any harm," said Anwen. "He did just save our lives, remember. But he's definitely covering for someone."

Cerys sprang out of her armchair and began pacing furiously up and down. "It has to be Flavia," she said. "She invited the Professor to the palace in the first place."

"And she's the one who sent Tonino up with the meals," said Anwen. "And blocked the maids from cleaning the room."

"Because she didn't want them to realize the Professor wasn't in there," said Cerys. "That's so devious!"

Anwen felt as if a great weight had lifted off her shoulders. She wasn't happy to be proved right about Tonino, but at least she didn't have to nurse her doubts alone anymore. It felt good to have Cerys on her side.

"So, the Professor killed King Thibault on Flavia's orders," said Cerys. "Then he escaped from the palace, and Tonino helped cover it up."

"Maybe," said Anwen. "All we know for sure is that the Professor wasn't in his room yesterday. We still can't prove he killed Thibault."

"You mean we need *more* proof? We're never going to solve this before tomorrow."

Anwen raised an eyebrow. "We?"

"I mean you," Cerys replied. "Although there's no way you can do it without me."

"Admit it," said Anwen, with a sly grin, "you care about this case almost as much as I do."

Cerys put her nose in the air. "I don't like being lied to, that's all," she said. "Whoever's behind this, I don't think they should get away with it."

"Me neither," said Anwen.

"So, what are we going to do about it?"

Anwen gave the question some thought. "First, we need to identify the killer," she said. "Our two suspects are the Chamberlain and Professor Umberto. Neither of them has an alibi, but neither of them has a clear motive either. Even if they were acting on orders from Flavia, murdering the king is a big step."

"All right," said Cerys. "How do we prove which one of them did it?"

"That's the second thing," said Anwen. "The killer moved Thibault's body out of the palace and dropped it into our world. That's such a strange thing to do, it has to be linked to their motive somehow. If we can figure out why they did it, that might point to our culprit."

"Is there a third thing?"

"Yes," said Anwen. "What did you mean earlier, when you said that I couldn't see what was right in front of me?"

Cerys gave her a pitying look. "You're the detective. You figure it out."

Anwen was trying to do just that when the Chamberlain strode into the nursery.

His cheeks were flushed, and beads of sweat stood out on his forehead. Cold and sickly dread swirled in Anwen's stomach as he squinted at them across the room—something was wrong.

"This has gone on long enough," he said, breathing heavily. "It's time to take care of you myself."

"Anwen?" Cerys retreated behind the cover of her armchair. "What's he talking about?"

The Chamberlain unhooked the golden mallet from his belt and weighed it in his hand. Anwen sprang to her feet and dragged Cerys out of the dollhouse. "Quick!" she said. "The mousehole!" They ran, but the Chamberlain's heavy footsteps crashed down behind them, closer and closer. They were barely halfway to the skirting board when Anwen realized they weren't going to make it in time.

16

Fight or Flight

Anwen and Cerys gripped hands as the Chamberlain bore down on them. The nursery trembled at his footsteps, and Anwen wondered how loud the mallet would be when it came whistling down to crush them. There was nowhere they could run to, and nowhere to hide.

"I can't allow this to continue," said the Chamberlain. He was so close that Anwen could have reached out to touch the toes of his shoes. She waited for the mallet to fall.

Instead, the Chamberlain set it down on the floor, got down on his knees, and lowered his ruddy, sweating face toward them.

"Do you know how embarrassing it is?" he said. "To have guests seeing the palace at its worst? I shudder to think what you're going to tell your people when you get home."

Anwen and Cerys exchanged a glance, and let go of each other's hands. Anwen activated her amplification spell.

"What do you mean?" she asked.

"Visiting dignitaries require the highest standards," he said. "But you've been left in a disused room, and with nothing but a clueless page boy to tend to you. Now even he's gone, so I'm here to take personal charge of your needs."

Cerys activated her own amplification spell. "Does that include snacks?"

Anwen waved her into silence. "Tonino's gone? Where?"

"Her Majesty has seen fit to send him on a personal errand outside the palace." The Chamberlain scowled. "He may be gone some time."

With all the questions surrounding Tonino's honesty, Anwen couldn't help but suspect the worst.

"Where is she sending him?"

"If it's none of my business, it's certainly none of yours," said the Chamberlain.

None of the Chamberlain's business? she thought. *That means Flavia's keeping secrets from him too. Interesting . . .*

"Name your requirements," said the Chamberlain. "Food, servants, entertainment. I can assure you—"

He winced suddenly, and clamped a hand to his head.

"What's wrong?" asked Anwen.

"Nothing," he snapped. "I just . . ." Before he could finish, he slumped sideways, hitting the floor so hard that Anwen fought to keep her balance.

"Is he dead?" asked Cerys.

As if in answer, the Chamberlain groaned.

"No, but this looks serious," said Anwen. "Come on."

They sprinted to the Chamberlain's head. His face was a rictus of pain, and he had worked his fingers underneath his periwig. Despite her dislike for the man, Anwen felt genuine concern.

"Is there anything we can do to help?" she asked.

"Nothing." The Chamberlain forced the word out through clenched teeth. "It'll pass."

Cerys cut her amplification spell. "Anwen, look!" she said. The Chamberlain's wig had slipped, revealing a shadowy patch of bare scalp beneath. "You wanted proof that he was in Thibault's room. This is our chance."

Cerys was right, Anwen realized. If the Chamberlain really was the murderer, and had been struck on the head by the same bust with which he had killed Thibault, then the proof was right in front of them.

They dashed forward, seized one of the wig's silver curls, and pulled. The wig fell away, revealing the Chamberlain's scalp in all its bald glory.

It was spotless. There was no injury, no bruising. Nothing at all.

"I don't understand," said Cerys. "There's supposed to be a big lump."

They jumped back as the Chamberlain struggled into a sitting position and fumbled something out of his pocket. It was a glass bottle, filled with a thick pink liquid, and Anwen got a good look at the label as he uncorked it and put it to his lips: DOCTOR PULASKI'S VALERIAN PAIN-AWAY. NOW WITH ADDED WILLOW AND GINGER ROOT!

"I know those ingredients," said Anwen. "Grandma and I use them for headache cures." She looked again at the Chamberlain as he guzzled mouthfuls of the medicine. "Do you get these migraines often?" she asked.

He squinted down at her, struggling to focus. "Temporary lapses," he said. "I'm in full control."

Anwen put her hands on her hips. She was no longer faced with a murder suspect but a difficult patient, and she knew exactly how to handle those. "How long has this been going on?" she asked. "And don't try fibbing."

The Chamberlain looked embarrassed. "You don't understand my position," he said. "I have a sense of authority to uphold. If the other servants ever found out . . ."

"Nothing you tell us will leave this room," said Anwen. "You have our word."

He peered at them doubtfully, until another wave of pain screwed his eyes shut. "I've always had them," he gasped. "But they got worse once King Thibault took the throne."

"Migraines are often caused by stress," said Anwen. "Did you find him difficult to work with?"

The Chamberlain grimaced. "That lazy, talentless, good-for-nothing . . ." He broke off to take another mouthful of medicine. "His father should have stuck to the plan and put Flavia on the throne instead."

Anwen gasped, and pulled out her notebook. "King Augustus was going to make Flavia queen? Doesn't the throne just pass to the eldest child?"

"Yes," said the Chamberlain. "But Flavia and Thibault are the same age."

Cerys reactivated her amplification spell. "Not even twins are exactly the same age," she said. "One's always born before the other."

The Chamberlain blinked heavily and wiped a dribble of medicine from his beard. "Cesarean section. Delivered simultaneously," he said. "So King Augustus had to choose. Was s'poshed to be Flavia, but Thibault had the public wrapped around his little finger with that blashted guitar."

"King Augustus changed his mind and appointed Thibault," said Anwen, her charcoal dancing over the page.

"It sounds to me like you're glad Thibault's gone," said Cerys.

"Whadaya 'mplying?" The Chamberlain raised the bottle to his lips again, but it slipped from his fingers. Anwen and Cerys had to jump back as it toppled over and spilled pink gunk over the carpet.

"Oopsh!" he said.

"He's drunk!" said Cerys.

Anwen sniffed a dollop of the medicine, and reeled back as her head began to spin.

"No," she said. "But valerian is a sedative, and this stuff's strong enough to knock a cart horse out cold."

"'m fiiiine," the Chamberlain burbled. "Jus' gimme a minute." He belched, snickered, then keeled over sideways and started snoring.

"Well," said Cerys. "He's not so stuck up now, is he?"

Anwen sighed, and canceled her amplification spell. "Imagine being in all that pain, but too afraid to tell anyone. Maybe that's why he's so horrible."

Cerys canceled her own spell again. "I wish he could have passed out *after* he brought us more breakfast," she said.

Anwen leafed through her last few pages of notes. "He did give us something," she said. "The migraines explain his mysterious disappearances. And he doesn't have a head injury, so he can't be the cause of the second bloodstain on the murder weapon."

"So he wasn't in Thibault's room after the concert?" asked Cerys.

"It seems unlikely," Anwen replied. "Which makes Professor Umberto our prime suspect."

"And Tonino's our only connection to him."

Anwen snapped the book shut. "Flavia's sending Tonino out on a secret errand. It *must* have something to do with the Professor. Maybe they know where he's hiding." She grabbed Cerys by the hand and pulled her in a run toward the window. "We might still have time."

"For what?" asked Cerys.

"To follow Tonino, of course." She looked down onto the parade ground. "There he is!"

Tonino was just stepping out through the palace gates as four guards held back the crowd of mourners. He paused, and cast a nervous look back toward the palace. Then he put his head down, and was swallowed by the crowd.

"We're too late," said Cerys.

"Not if we fly," Anwen replied.

Cerys took in the sickening drop to the parade ground. "I don't know any flight spells!"

"Who said anything about spells?" said Anwen. "Go and fetch me one of those pastries."

"Get one yourself if you're hungry."

Anwen groaned. "Not for me, stupid. For the pigeon."

She pointed along the balcony to where a plump gray pigeon with an iridescent-green breast sat on the casement. It was ignoring them, but surveying the inside of the nursery with open curiosity.

"Why do I get the feeling I'm going to regret this?" said Cerys. She jogged back inside, and returned a moment later with a squashed cake, which she handed to Anwen.

"Hello," said Anwen, waving the cake in the air. "We've got some breakfast for you."

The bird cocked its head and peered down at them. Then it launched off the casement, described a graceful circle in the air, and landed with a snap of its wings beside them.

Cerys made a nervous sound in her throat, and even Anwen shrank back a little—the pigeon was taller than a shire horse, and its beak, which had looked so harmless from a distance, suddenly seemed more threatening.

The creature puffed out its chest and cooed.

"Help yourself," Anwen replied. She dropped the cake at its feet; the pigeon pecked it up in a few swift movements, then cooed again.

"Your name's Archimboldo?" asked Anwen. "I'm Anwen, and this is Cerys."

Archimboldo strutted past them into the nursery, where he turned in a slow circle, cooing animatedly.

"What's the matter?" asked Cerys.

"He likes the murals," said Anwen. "But he thinks the artist should have used a more naturalistic style, and the brushstrokes are a bit heavy-handed."

Archimboldo cooed again.

"Also, he thinks they should have added some pigeons."

Cerys looked at her blankly. "He's an art critic?"

"Apparently." Anwen jogged to Archimboldo's side. "It's true, you don't see enough pigeons in art, and we'd love to discuss it with you, but we're really hoping you can give us a lift outside. It's an emergency."

"I'm not riding a pigeon," Cerys protested. "They eat out of dustbins."

Archimboldo cooed and bobbed his head.

"He says he'll do it," said Anwen. "As long as we agree to listen to his thoughts on composition of form in modern sculpture."

“Right now?” asked Cerys. “Because Tonino’s getting away.”

Archimboldo lowered his belly to the ground, and allowed Anwen to climb onto his back. He felt remarkably fragile beneath her, and she worried that he might not be able to carry both her and Cerys, but when he stood up and flapped his wings, all her doubts disappeared. He hopped through the air and was at Cerys’s side in a second. Anwen giggled—it felt as if she had flown there herself.

“Get on,” she said.

“I can’t believe you’re making me do this,” said Cerys. She climbed up and wrapped her arms tightly around Anwen’s waist. “First mice and now bir—Aaaaaaaaarghh!”

She screamed as Archimboldo launched himself out the window. Suddenly there was nothing but empty air beneath them, and the rush of wind in their faces. Anwen felt as if she had left her stomach behind in the nursery, but she was too excited to be scared—they were getting closer to Thibault’s killer. The answers were out there, hidden somewhere in the city, and with Archimboldo’s help, Tonino might lead her right to them.

17
Flight into Mystery

Cerys clung to Anwen, and Anwen clung to Archimboldo, as the pigeon circled above the piazza.

From this height, Anwen could almost imagine that the crowds of mourners outside the palace, or the teams of workers clearing the ruins of the monument, were normal-sized people. Unfortunately, none of them looked like Tonino.

"I think we've lost him," she shouted, her words snatched away by the wind rushing past them.

Then a glint of light drew her eye—not Tonino, but the shine of a soldier's helmet, heading away from the monument. "Who's that?" she said, pointing.

Archimboldo dove, so steep and fast that both girls screamed at the top of their lungs. When Anwen was sure that he was going to nosedive straight into the marble, he pulled up and swooped low over the heads of the crowd. To her surprise, the helmet belonged to the Captain, and, ahead of him, through the press of bodies, she finally saw Tonino's telltale tricorn hat. He was hurrying out of the piazza into a tree-lined boulevard thronged with people.

"It looks like we're not the only ones who want to know what Tonino's up to," she said. "Don't lose them."

Archimboldo cooed in acknowledgment and rose higher with a few powerful snaps of his wings.

"This is worse than being on the beanstalk," said Cerys.

Once they were higher than the surrounding buildings, Anwen got a real sense of the giants' city. Broad avenues radiated outward from the piazza, linked by a fractured pattern of narrow streets that wound between the golden rooftops of the grand old buildings. For a moment, all the cares of the investigation fell away, and she simply thrilled at the feeling of freedom. There was a whole new world for her to explore, and, with Archimboldo's help, she and Cerys could go anywhere. It was glorious.

Cerys's grip around her waist brought her back to the moment. Archimboldo followed Tonino's hat as it bobbed along the boulevard. It obviously marked him out as palace staff, because Anwen could see people doffing their own hats as he passed by. They also hailed the Captain behind him, and it wasn't long before Tonino looked back over his shoulder. He and the Captain both came to a stop as their eyes met.

"Oh no!" said Anwen. "We need to do something."

"Why?" asked Cerys.

"Because Tonino won't go to wherever Princess Flavia sent him if he knows he's being followed," Anwen replied. "We've got to help him get away."

"How are we supposed to do that?"

Anwen didn't know. They had to find some way to distract the Captain without giving themselves away—if Tonino saw them, he would definitely abandon his mission. But what could they do to help? They were just two girls and a . . .

. . . and a bird.

The idea came to her in a flash, and she leaned forward to whisper it in Archimboldo's ear. He gave a judgmental cluck in response.

"I don't care if it's crass," Anwen replied. "It's urgent. Please! We'll listen to as many art lectures as you want."

Archimboldo banked again and spiraled down toward the street until he was a few yards above the Captain. Anwen saw the Captain raise a finger to point at Tonino, and then Archimboldo released a large, wet dropping right down the front of his breastplate.

The Captain stared in shock at the mess on his uniform, then up into the sky. He locked eyes with

Anwen for an instant, before a second dropping hit him square in the face.

I'm so sorry! Anwen thought. "Good shot, Archimboldo."

Archimboldo climbed again as the Captain wiped the guano from his eyes. At the same time, Tonino turned and ran, ducking around the nearest corner. The Captain took a few steps after him, but by the time he reached the junction, Tonino had crossed the street and slipped out of sight down an alleyway.

"Thank you," said Anwen, hugging Archimboldo's neck.

"Is this your answer to every problem?" said Cerys. "Persuade a bird to poo on it for you?"

"I wouldn't have thought of it if you hadn't been here," said Anwen.

"If I'm supposed to feel flattered, I don't," said Cerys. "Not after you and your pet seagull spent a week terrorizing me."

"Colin's not a pet; he's a wild animal."

Whatever comeback Cerys had been preparing lodged in her throat. "The seagull's called Colin?"

"Not really," said Anwen. "But if you ask a seagull what they call themselves, the answer's always either 'cross' or 'hungry.' So I called mine Colin."

Cerys stared blankly at her. "That's the most ridiculous thing I've ever heard."

Archimboldo carried them over the rooftops to a small, leafy square, where Tonino emerged from the alley. He headed straight to the entrance of a wonky old brick building, topped with a haphazard jumble of turrets and peaked roofs. A gold sign above the door read ROYAL SCHOOL OF THE ARTS.

"Isn't this the place that turned down Marcus and the Captain?" asked Cerys.

"You're right," said Anwen. "And it's where the Maestro teaches."

"Who?"

"Thibault and Flavia's old music tutor," said Anwen. "The one who accused Thibault of faking his talent."

Why would Flavia send Tonino here? Anwen wondered as Archimboldo brought them in for a landing on top of the school. The jumble of roofs surrounded them like a mountain range, broken up by large skylights, some of which were propped open. Music and conversation drifted out of them, borne aloft on the summer breeze.

Anwen and Cerys slid off Archimboldo's back. The roof was hot to the touch and radiated heat like an oven.

"Now what do we do?" said Cerys, fanning herself with her hand. "Search the whole building?"

"I don't have any better ideas," said Anwen.

They struck off uphill to the nearest skylight. Through it, they saw a large art studio, in which a group of young giants were painting a still life of fruit and flowers. They hurried past it to the next window—this was a pottery workshop, the students all up to their elbows in wet clay.

"This is why that bird knows so much about art," said Cerys. "He spends all day up here watching the classes."

Anwen paused to wipe sweat from her eyes. "Tonino's not here for art," she said. "If this place has anything to do with Thibault's murder, the connection has to be musical."

Cerys closed her eyes and listened. "Over there," she said. A discordant dirge emanated from a skylight several rooftops away. Anwen couldn't tell whether it was a chorus of flutes being played very badly, or someone trying to bathe a group of cats.

"It's worth a shot," she said.

They were both sweaty and exhausted by the time they reached the skylight. Below them, a trio of students was attempting to play their way through a recorder concerto for their tutor, who had her fingers in her ears. The room next door was full of gigantic harps, as tall as oak trees, standing in a circle, waiting for a lesson to begin.

"We're close," said Anwen. "I know it."

They were in the shadow of a circular tower now, jutting up from the corner of the building. There was a small window set into its side—too high to see into from where they stood, but the brickwork was rough and pitted, and it proved to be an easy climb. They reached the sill and found the window ajar.

Inside was a circular study, lined with bookshelves and musical instruments of every kind. A desk was covered with papers and a half-empty cup of tea, which was growing a skin.

"Nothing," said Cerys.

Anwen was about to admit defeat when the study door opened. Tonino entered, followed by a slender elderly woman with a tight bun of silver hair. She did not look amused.

"Satisfied?" said the woman, gesturing to the empty room. "As I told you, there's been no sign of the Maestro for two days. I'd be happy to see the back of him if he hadn't dumped his teaching duties on me."

"But Maestra Bellini," said Tonino, "when *exactly* did he disappear?"

"A few hours after your last visit," she replied.

"I don't know what you spoke about, but once you left, he wouldn't stop crowing about his ludicrous theory that King Thibault was using magic to create his music. He wanted to unmask him at the concert, in front of the whole kingdom."

Tonino looked stunned. "With what proof?"

"A rare book, apparently," said Maestra Bellini. "Between you and me, most of us stopped taking the Maestro seriously some time ago. He's a brilliant musician, but he's let his obsession with the king consume him. I hope he didn't cause a scene at the concert."

Tonino frowned. "There was no sign of him."

"Perhaps he got cold feet," said Maestra Bellini. "It wouldn't surprise me if he stormed off to nurse his ego, but he certainly hasn't come back here."

Even from her vantage point on the windowsill, Anwen could see the mounting look of disquiet on Tonino's face. "Her Majesty wants you to let her know immediately if the Maestro makes contact."

"Certainly," said Maestra Bellini. "May I ask, does this have anything to do with King Thibault's death?"

Tonino went white. "I hope not."

She followed him from the room, leaving Anwen and Cerys openmouthed with astonishment on the windowsill.

"Marcus was right," said Cerys. "Whatever's going on here, Tonino's part of it."

"Maybe," said Anwen. She fought to make sense of what they had just heard. Did any of it connect with what they already knew?

"He must be," said Cerys. "The Maestro had a vendetta against Thibault, and Flavia sent Tonino here to meet with him on the day of the concert. That's just a few hours before the murder!"

"But we've got no proof that the Maestro wanted to hurt Thibault," Anwen replied. "It sounds like he just wanted to expose him for somehow faking his talent. And how could the Maestro get close enough to commit murder if he was banned from the palace?"

Cerys pouted. "All right then, genius, what do you think happened?"

"I don't know," said Anwen. "But this is a third disappearance to add to Thibault's and Professor Umberto's, and all three of them are linked to the concert." She began pacing along the sill. "Thibault was there performing, Professor Umberto was there to listen, and the Maestro went to try and convince people it was fake. It's all about the music . . ."

"I don't want to hurry you," said Cerys, "but Tonino's already on his way back to the palace. If we're not there when he arrives, he'll know we've been up to something."

Anwen battered the palms of her hands against her forehead, hoping to dislodge some insight. "We can beat Tonino back on Archimboldo," she said. "But first, I want to take a look at the Maestro's office."

"To find what?"

"I don't know yet," said Anwen. "I'll tell you when we find it."

18

A Musical Mystery

Anwen and Cerys slipped into the Maestro's office through the open window. Although they were high up, they found an easy path along the dusty top of a bookcase, onto a set of robes hanging from an adjacent hatstand. They slid down the velvet folds, decorated with a pattern of gold and white musical clefs, into a capacious pocket, and from there it was a short jump onto the Maestro's desk.

"Look for anything connected to the palace," said Anwen as they split up. "Tonino came here to speak to the Maestro before the concert, so he might have brought something with him. Or the Maestro might have made notes."

"Why don't we just go back to the palace and ask Tonino to his face?" said Cerys.

"Because he might not tell us the truth," said Anwen. "And if he is involved in the murder, we'd be putting ourselves in danger."

"I think we're already in danger," Cerys muttered, but continued across the desk, stopping to read the scattered papers beneath her feet. "This is all just sheet music and class registers," she said. "Boring."

Anwen hurried from sheet to sheet at her own end of the desk. "Same here," she said. "Let's check the rest of the room."

Stacks of old books were piled against the desk, forming a neat staircase down to the carpet. Anwen made for the bookcase, while Cerys headed in the opposite direction, toward an old chest and some more piles of paperwork.

Anwen's frustration grew as she scanned the titles on the shelves. They were all dry, academic works about music history and theory—nothing that might suggest a link to Thibault. There was something about them that made her pause, though—each book's spine was cracked and worn with use. She thought back to the bookcase in Thibault's room, and how shiny and pristine each volume on the shelves had been.

The Maestro reads his books, but Thibault didn't, she thought. *Is that relevant?*

She moved on, and had just spotted something in the small fireplace when Cerys called to her.

"I've found something strange."

Anwen joined her. Cerys pointed to something that looked like a large, hairy caterpillar on the floor, about five feet in length. It took a few seconds for Anwen to realize what it was.

"A fake mustache?" she said.

"There are more," said Cerys. "Look." She pointed to a slender wooden case nearby. A sliding drawer protruded from its side, revealing more furry tufts.

"Help me with it," said Anwen, and together they pulled the drawer open, revealing a sunken bed of different mustaches, sideburns, and beards, of varying styles and colors. A label attached to the drawer read GENTLEMAN'S NOVELTY FACIAL HAIR KIT. AMUSE YOUR FRIENDS AT WHIMSICAL SOIRÉES!

"What's a music teacher doing with this?" asked Cerys.

"I don't know," said Anwen. "But there's something missing. See?" She pointed to an empty space in the drawer, beneath the label SAGE'S BEARD, GRAY.

"A disguise," said Cerys. "Maybe he planned to sneak into the palace."

"Good thinking," said Anwen. "But if he could do that, and he really had proof that Thibault was faking his musical talent, why didn't he use it?"

"Perhaps something happened to him before he got the chance."

Anwen snapped her fingers. "There's one more thing I need to check." She sprinted back to the fireplace, which was cold and empty except for a pile of ashes and a few charred scraps of paper. "Someone lit a fire here recently," she said, wading knee-deep into the ash. "That's a bit unusual for the middle of summer, isn't it?" She gathered up the bits of paper before kicking her way back onto the carpet. "I knew I'd seen something on here," she said, laying the scraps out in front of her and brushing the ash from them.

"Writing," said Cerys.

"I think it's a letter, or what's left of one," said Anwen. "A letter the Maestro didn't want anyone else to read."

The topmost fragment was curled and blackened at the edges, but the symbol of a crown was still visible beneath the damage.

"Headed notepaper," said Anwen. "This came from the palace."

Cerys helped her brush off the other scraps. "What do they say?"

Only a few words had survived the flames, and it was impossible to tell which order they came in, but Anwen and Cerys arranged them until they made some sort of sense.

—y dearest Maes—
—growing concern that my brother has—
—require your help to—
—for the sake of my family's reputation—

Anwen was openmouthed. "This has to be from Flavia," she said. "She had some sort of problem with Thibault, and turned to the Maestro for help."

"No wonder she wanted to keep it secret," said Cerys. "Asking for help from your brother's worst enemy isn't a good look. But help with what?"

Anwen folded up the scraps of paper and tucked them under her arm. "I'm not sure. Maybe she thought Thibault was a fraud as well."

"So they plotted to humiliate him in front of the whole kingdom?" said Cerys. "That doesn't sound like the sort of thing a good sister would do."

Anwen's skin prickled. She hated to think that anyone could do something so cruel to their own family. "I'm starting to think that Flavia is a very *bad* sister," she said. "But this answers some of our other questions."

"Which ones?"

They were interrupted by a tapping sound from the window and looked up to see Archimboldo pecking the glass. He made an inquisitive cooing sound.

"I'll explain everything back at the nursery," Anwen replied. "Sorry to keep you waiting, Archimboldo. Yes, we're ready to leave. And you can tell us all about modern sculpture on the way."

19

Letter from the Heavens

Stone dust rained down from the sky, catching the afternoon sun. Eira watched it settle on the fields from a stool outside her front door.

"About time," she said. The door beside her opened, and Meredith stepped out, stirring a cup of tea.

"What's going on now?" Meredith asked.

"Movement in the Sky Kingdom," Eira replied. "My guess is they're getting ready to take back their dead."

Meredith watched the last of the dust settle, glittering like ice crystals. "Do you think they'll bring back Anwen and the Powell girl?"

"They'd better," Eira replied. With the giant cuff link safely stowed inside the cottage and the Old Stumpers all taken care of for the moment, she'd had nothing to do all day but fret about Anwen and Cerys, and it had done nothing for her patience.

They watched the sky in silence, until the sound of running footsteps from the road made them turn. A red-faced Stillpike appeared, his guitar slung over his back.

“Are the brutes invading?” he said.

“Are you here to stop them if they do?” asked Meredith.

“I’d put up a fight,” said Stillpike, striking a noble pose that was only slightly undermined by the flop of sweaty hair in his eyes. “I’m not afraid to risk all in the defense of life, liberty, and a hot dinner. Speaking of which . . .”

Eira tutted. “There’s fresh bacon in the pan and tea in the pot,” she said, hooking a thumb at the front door. “Help yourself.”

“M’lady.” Stillpike scurried inside, reemerging a minute later with a steaming mug of tea and a bacon sandwich, dripping fat.

“So,” he said through a mouthful of food, “what do we think they’re plotting?”

As if in answer to his question, a dark shape materialized in the sky.

“Is that a balloon?” said Meredith, shielding her eyes against the sun.

It was a parachute, Eira saw as it sank toward them—roughly thirty feet across, with something suspended beneath it on lengths of giant string as thick as ship’s ropes.

“We won’t get any answers sitting here,” she said.

They hurried around the feet of the fallen giant to the field where the new beanstalk had briefly stood. The parachute was about a thousand feet above them now, and Eira saw that it was actually a giant handkerchief made of golden silk. The thing beneath it was a boulder—although it was probably little more than a pebble to the giants—with a folded sheet of giant paper tied to it.

The rock touched down with a soft thump in the middle of the field, and the handkerchief settled over them all.

"Pure gold thread," said Stillpike, stroking the fabric almost lovingly. "It must be worth a fortune."

"I couldn't care less," said Eira. With Meredith's help, she detached the paper from the stone and, together, the three of them dragged it out into the daylight.

"It's a letter," said Eira. Once unfolded, the note was roughly the size of three large bedsheets stitched together.

"Get a paper cut from this and you could lose a hand," said Meredith, but Eira didn't reply. She was already reading the crimson handwriting.

People of Old Stump,

Her Majesty, Queen Flavia Thunderstride, was greatly saddened to hear of the destruction of your village. The body that fell on it was that of her brother, the late King Thibault Thunderstride, and steps will be taken to retrieve his remains at dawn tomorrow. Two of your villagers, Anwen Sludge and Cerys Piffell, will also be returned to you unharmed.

Sincerely,

Genaro Agosti, Royal Chamberlain

"We should demand compensation for the damage," said Meredith.

"Good idea," said Stillpike. "Let's squeeze them for every penny they've got."

"Shush, both of you," snapped Eira. "There's more here, look."

Beneath the Chamberlain's signature was a note written at human scale, and in Anwen's handwriting.

Dear Grandma,

Hello from the Sky Kingdom! The giants are taking good care of us—Cerys is eating enough for three people, and I'm trying to do my duty as a Meadow Witch. I still have lots of questions to answer before we get home.

All my love,

Anwen x

Eira sat back on the grass with a deep sigh of relief. "They're both safe," she said. "Thank goodness."

"I knew they would be," said Meredith, hugging her.

Stillpike examined the letter over her shoulder. "A king, eh?" he said. "It's been a while since we had any fancy visitors around here."

"He's not exactly a tourist," said Eira. "Kings are bad news when they're alive, but dead ones can cause even more trouble. It sounds like Anwen's trying to get to the bottom of things, though. I'd better get word to her about that cuff link."

"Say again?" asked Stillpike.

"We found a giant cuff link in the wreckage yesterday," said Meredith. "We checked, and it didn't come from our dead king here, so it might have come from whoever killed him."

Stillpike teased the ends of his mustache between his fingers and thumbs. "Interesting," he said. "A trail of clues, eh?"

"One clue, perhaps," said Eira. "But maybe Anwen can find a use for it."

"How are you going to get word to her?" asked Meredith.

"With a little help from a friend of hers," said Eira. "I know just who to ask."

20

Confession and Contrition

Archimboldo flew Anwen and Cerys back through the open nursery window, and almost straight into the irate features of the Captain.

The girls screamed as Archimboldo banked sharply, performed a barrel roll, and landed in a fluster of feathers in front of Fortune Hall. They half climbed, half fell off him onto the carpet.

"Busy morning?" asked the Captain.

The Chamberlain lay between them, mouth open, snoring steadily. The Captain nudged him with his foot.

"I assume this is your doing," he said.

"No," Anwen replied, gathering up the scraps of paper she'd carried back from the Maestro's fireplace. "He took too much headache medicine. He'll recover soon."

The Captain grunted and tapped his breastplate, which was encrusted with dried bird droppings. "This was you, though."

"You can't prove anything!" said Cerys.

"He just watched us fly in on a pigeon," said Anwen. "I don't think he needs any more proof."

"I should arrest you both for interfering with an investigation," he said. "What were you doing outside the palace? And on a bird!" He gestured at Archimboldo, who grabbed a few pastries in his beak and flapped up onto the roof of Fortune Hall with them. "What if you'd fallen off? I'm supposed to be keeping you safe."

With a guilty start, Anwen realized that she hadn't even considered this. "We're sorry," she said. "About sneaking out, and the pigeon poo. But Tonino saw you following him, and we had to give him a chance to get away."

"So we could follow him instead," said Cerys.

"That's my job, not yours," he replied.

"Don't you want to know where he went?" asked Cerys.

A muscle in the Captain's jaw flexed. His nostrils flared. "You found out?"

"We did," said Anwen proudly.

"And we got very hot and sticky doing it," said Cerys. "So, if you'll excuse me, I'm going to get changed." She walked through the open front of Fortune Hall and upstairs to her room. "A little privacy, please?"

The Captain closed the dollhouse up for her. "All right," he said. "I don't like that you did it, but now it's done, tell me where he went."

"To the Royal School of the Arts, looking for the Maestro."

The Captain's eyebrows shot up. "The Maestro! What's he got to do with all this?"

"I have a theory," Anwen replied. "But before I share it with you, I need you to tell me everything you know about Professor Umberto."

A fly buzzed in through the nursery window and began circling the Captain's head. He waved it away as he considered his answer. "He was an older man, maybe in his sixties. Shortish, roundish, well dressed. Red spectacles, and a top hat."

"And a beard?" asked Anwen.

"Yes, a big bushy silver one," he replied. "How did you know?"

Anwen raised a finger, motioning for him to wait. "And what about his background? Did you check it?"

The Captain shook his head. "Her Majesty only announced his visit a few hours before he arrived, so there wasn't time. I've written to the governor of the Long Lakes region, but that's five days' journey north of here. I won't get any confirmation for weeks."

Anwen added this as a note in her book. "I don't think you'll get any at all," she said. "Because I don't think Professor Umberto ever existed."

The Captain looked dumbfounded, but before he

could reply, the nursery door opened to reveal Tonino. The page boy froze, his eyes flicking from the Captain to Anwen and finally to the slumbering form of the Chamberlain.

"Tonino," said the Captain. "We need to talk."

Tonino moved as if his feet were made of lead, and settled himself on the toy chest. "Yes, sir?"

"The palace is in lockdown," said the Captain, waving away the fly again. "But Her Majesty sent you outside. It must have been for something very important."

"Yes. I mean, I think so."

"Where did she send you?"

Tonino squirmed. "I'm not allowed to say."

Anwen sat down on the front step of Fortune Hall, listening intently.

"At least you're not stupid enough to try lying to me this time," said the Captain. "I already know you were at the School of the Arts."

"You followed me?" said Tonino.

"No," said Anwen. "Cerys and I did. And we overheard your conversation with Maestra Bellini too."

All the color drained from Tonino's face.

"The Maestro's been missing since the day of the concert," Anwen continued. "The same day Flavia sent you to him with a letter, asking for help."

The Captain looked between them both with a mixture of shock and anger. "She did what?"

"I didn't know!" Tonino said. "I delivered the letter, but it was confidential. I never found out what it said."

"How do *you* know what was in it?" the Captain asked Anwen.

"We found these scraps in his office fireplace." She offered him the charred pieces of paper. "Thibault was causing some sort of problem, and Flavia thought the Maestro could help her solve it," she explained as the Captain took the scraps and read them one by one. "After Tonino's visit, the Maestro told everyone at the school that he was going to expose Thibault as a fraud during the concert, and that he had a book containing all the proof he needed."

The furrows in the Captain's brow deepened. "He was still convinced that Thibault's guitar was enchanted," he said. "But why would Queen Flavia want to help him? She knows giants and magic don't mix."

"Aren't we forgetting something here?" Cerys's voice made them all turn, and she stepped out of Fortune Hall wearing a gold sequined three-piece suit, complete with top hat and tails. "Whether the guitar is magic or not, the Maestro never actually made it into the palace to find out."

"What if he did?" Anwen replied.

"Impossible," said the Captain. "He's barred for life. We wouldn't even let him through the front gate."

"I think that's exactly what you did," said Anwen.

Cerys pressed a hand to Anwen's forehead. "Are you feeling well? Because you're not making any sense."

Anwen swatted the hand away. "You want to be a glamourist, so think like one. Someone's been fooling us. The answer's obvious if you look beneath the surface."

"If you already know the answer, why don't you just tell us?" said Cerys.

"Because this is more fun," said Anwen. "Two musical experts have gone missing: the Maestro and Professor Umberto. They both received invitations from Queen Flavia, and they were both supposed to be at Thibault's concert, but didn't make it. I thought it was too strange to be a coincidence, but now I'm sure."

Cerys thought for a moment, before her face brightened. "The disguise kit we found in the Maestro's office," she said. "Professor Umberto was the Maestro all along!"

"What?" said Tonino and the Captain together.

Anwen couldn't tell which of them looked more surprised.

"I told you the Professor didn't really exist, Captain," she said. "I think Queen Flavia invented a history for him that would be difficult for you to check."

"I admit, I'm impressed with the misdirection," said Cerys. "But that means—" Before she could say any more, something knocked the top hat from her head with a wet splat. She picked it up, only to find it coated in a thick yellowish gloop. She sniffed it, gagged, and threw it back on the floor. "Bird poo!"

Anwen looked up in confusion. The poo was too small to have come from Archimboldo, who was still perched on top of the dollhouse, but where else could it have come from? Then she noticed the fly flitting around the Captain's face. She looked closer. "Colin!" she cried.

The black speck paused, then spiraled down toward her until it was no longer a speck but a very cross-looking seagull. Colin landed in her hands and nipped weakly at her fingers.

"Wow, is that a bird from your world?" asked Tonino. "He's minute!"

"He must have flown up through the thin place," said Anwen. "No wonder he's exhausted, poor thing."

"Poor thing?" said Cerys. "That filthy creature is haunting me!"

"Sorry," said Anwen. "I never thought he'd follow us all the way up here. It's quite impressive, if you think about it."

Colin cawed, and it was then that Anwen noticed the slip of paper tied around his leg.

"What's this?"

She detached the paper and unrolled it, and immediately recognized her grandmother's handwriting.

Dear Anwen,
Received your note. Glad all well. Found a piece of evidence down here—giant gold cuff link with music motif (see drawing). Was NOT from the victim. Possibly from killer or witness? Hope this helps.

Love,
Grandma

P.S. Cerys's parents send her their love also.

Anwen read the note out loud, then pressed it to her heart—her grandmother and Old Stump suddenly felt much closer. "This is important," she said. "If the cuff link belongs to the Maestro, it's the physical proof we need to tie him to Thibault's murder."

"Agreed," said the Captain. "But I assume he's still wearing the other one, so we can't prove it without finding him."

Anwen pursed her lips. "Tonino? Was he wearing these cuff links when you met with him?"

"I'm sorry," Tonino replied. "I didn't notice."

"Then it's a good thing one of us was paying attention in that office," said Cerys, looking very smug indeed. "Don't tell me you didn't notice, Anwen."

"Notice what?" Anwen replied.

"We saw this exact design close up," said Cerys. "It was printed all over the Maestro's robes—the ones we used to climb down from his office window. I bet they were part of a matching set."

"You noticed that?" said Anwen.

"What can I say?" Cerys replied. "I take an interest in fashion."

"All right," said the Captain. "The cuff link definitely ties the Maestro to the killing."

"That means his travel sickness at dinner was all an act as well," said Tonino.

"Definitely," said Anwen. "It must have been an excuse to leave the table early, but what happened after that is still a mystery. I'm quite sure he didn't go to his guest room, though. That's why it was so tidy."

All eyes turned to Tonino, who looked shamefacedly at the carpet. "I'm really sorry," he said. "I had no idea the Professor was really the Maestro. And I didn't want to lie about speaking to him in his room."

"Then why did you?" said the Captain.

"Her Majesty told me that the Professor wasn't just travel sick, he had a serious illness," said Tonino. "He didn't want anyone to know, though, so she'd sent him to the royal hospital in secret. She told me to take his meals to his room and eat them myself, so nobody would suspect that anything was wrong." He looked around the circle of faces. "I thought I was helping."

"That explains why there were only grapes left on the plate we found in the guest room," said Anwen.

Tonino grimaced. "I've never liked them. They're too squishy."

The Captain held up a hand for silence. "If Professor Umberto—I mean, the Maestro—didn't go to his own room after dinner, there's only one place he would have gone. Thibault's chambers."

"But they were always locked," said Tonino.

"And Marcus was in there a few minutes before

the concert started, to polish the guitar," said Cerys. "He didn't see anyone except Thibault."

"Maybe Flavia slipped the Maestro a key," said Anwen. "If he let himself in while Thibault was still downstairs eating dinner, he would have had plenty of time to hide somewhere out of sight. Maybe under the bed, or in the wardrobe."

The Captain nodded. "Flavia wouldn't have trouble getting hold of a key. Now we just need to find out what went wrong."

"What do you mean?" asked Anwen.

"If the Maestro was only there to expose Thibault as a fake, why did he end up killing him?" the Captain replied.

"And why wait so long to do it?" asked Cerys. "The Maestro could have killed Thibault as soon as he came upstairs from dinner, instead of hiding in a cupboard for two hours and waiting for the concert to finish."

This was a good question, and Anwen didn't have an answer. Even though she was certain that the Maestro was the killer, there were still some troubling gaps in the puzzle. "The only person who can tell us what happened is the Maestro himself," she said.

"Not quite," said the Captain. "I have to confront Queen Flavia."

Tonino's mouth dropped open. "How? She's the queen."

"But she's not above the law," the Captain replied. "She's lied to us both, and suppressed evidence. I hate to say it, but she's now a suspected accomplice in her brother's murder."

Heavy silence filled the room, until Cerys broke it.

"Told you so!"

"Cerys," said Anwen. "Now is not the time."

The Captain prodded the Chamberlain with his toe again. "We should take him with us," he said. "As the queen's highest official, he needs to hear everything we've got to say. Tonino, can you carry Anwen and Cerys, please? They'll need to present their evidence to the court too."

Clearly relieved to be trusted with some responsibility again, Tonino removed his hat and helped the girls climb into it. Meanwhile, the Captain hauled the Chamberlain upright and took him under the arms.

Archimboldo wolfed down the last of his stolen pastries and cooed quizzically.

"Leave some for the mice," Anwen told him as she cradled Colin. "And don't poo on the dollhouse!"

The group set off for the throne room.

"How do you think Flavia's going to take it?" asked Cerys.

"I don't know," said Anwen. "How would you react?"

"Badly."

Anwen chewed her lip nervously. What if Flavia didn't want to come quietly? She had a kingdom full of giants at her command, while she and Cerys had one soldier, a teenage boy, and an unconscious snob on their side.

You also have the truth, she thought in an echo of her grandmother's voice. She hoped it would be enough.

21

The Moment of Truth

Their group drew a lot of odd stares as they made their way through the palace—Tonino, pale and nervous, carrying Anwen and Cerys in his hat; Anwen cradling Colin; and the Captain dragging the Chamberlain, still snoring, by the armpits. In fact, quite a crowd had gathered around them by the time they reached the throne room doors. Anwen saw Marcus and Gabriela among them.

"Cato? What's going on?" asked Marcus.

"I'll explain later," the Captain replied. "Help me with the doors. We need to see Queen Flavia immediately."

"We've solved the murder!" announced Cerys, addressing the onlookers like a showman at a village fair. Anwen pulled her down into the hat as the crowd buzzed with excited conversation.

"No, we haven't," she hissed. "We still don't know exactly what happened."

"But we're about to find out," Cerys replied. "You should be happy."

"I'll be happy if Queen Flavia actually gives us the answers we need, and doesn't just have us executed."

Cerys's confidence faltered. "She wouldn't."

Anwen could guess what Cerys was thinking—there were guards posted throughout the great hallway, looking increasingly jumpy as the crowd's agitation grew. When the time came to choose, would they remain loyal to their Captain, or their queen?

"Captain," said Anwen as Marcus shouldered the great doors open. "Maybe we should bring all these people with us. As witnesses."

"Safety in numbers," he said. "Good idea." As Marcus helped him support the Chamberlain, he called to the nearest guards. "Get everyone here into the throne room. They all need to hear what we've got to say."

Their group reached the throne at the head of the crowd. Queen Flavia, still surrounded by her clerks and attendants, rose imperiously to her feet.

"What is the meaning of this, Captain?"

"Your Majesty," he replied. "You lied to me."

The room fell deathly silent. A muscle in Flavia's cheek twitched.

"You found out," she said quietly.

"Actually, Anwen and Cerys did," he replied. "Perhaps they should explain."

Anwen flinched at the sudden attention, but cleared her throat. "We know that Professor Umberto was really the Maestro," she said. "You invited him to the palace, in disguise, on the night of Thibault's concert, and he's been missing ever since. We're sure he murdered your brother."

The crowd erupted in uproar, and it was several seconds before Flavia could make herself heard.

"I'm sure too," she said.

"Then why didn't you tell me?" the Captain demanded.

Flavia sat down heavily and put her head in her hands. "I'm sorry," she said. "I should have, I know, but everything happened so quickly. I panicked, and . . ." Her eyes shone with repressed tears for an instant. Then she blinked, and the facade of calm assurance dropped back into place. "I made some poor decisions," she said. "But I never meant Thibault any harm."

"Then why did you help his worst enemy sneak into the palace?" asked Cerys.

"Because the Maestro saw what everyone else refused to see," said Flavia. "My brother had no interest in music. He never managed more than a tuneless dirge in over a decade of lessons, but the moment he found that guitar in the attic, he became the most accomplished musician in the kingdom."

"You think Thibault was faking his musical skills," said Anwen.

"Wouldn't you be suspicious?" asked Flavia.

Anwen didn't answer, because she didn't want to admit that she almost certainly would be.

"I didn't know how he was doing it," Flavia said. "So I reached out to the Maestro for help."

"The letter you had me deliver," said Tonino.

She nodded. "I knew the Maestro would need to see the guitar in action, up close. The concert seemed like the perfect opportunity."

The Captain's expression was grim. "You wanted to humiliate your brother," he said.

"No," Flavia replied. "I wanted him to stand aside quietly, and let me take the throne instead."

"Blackmail," said the Captain.

"Fairness," Flavia replied. "The throne was going to be mine, until Thibault became such a huge star that our father changed his mind. Thibault lied to him, and to the people. He cheated me out of my inheritance."

Anwen swallowed her anxiety. "That sounds like a good motive for murder," she said.

Flavia fixed her with a piercing stare. "I don't pretend that I liked my brother. But murder was never the plan."

"What went wrong?" asked the Captain.

"I don't know," Flavia replied. "The Maestro camc to the palace in the guise of Professor Umberto.

He made his excuses during dinner, and left the table to sneak into Thibault's room with a master key I'd given him. He was going to hide there until the concert began, and spy on Thibault performing. He claimed that would tell him everything he needed to know about exactly how the guitar was enchanted. Once he had his answer, he'd tell me everything."

"But he never came back," said Anwen.

"No," said Flavia. "The concert finished, and there was still no sign of him. I was sure he couldn't have left the palace without being seen, but he was still missing the following morning. Then I learned that Thibault had vanished as well."

The Captain drew in a long, weary breath. "The fact that you didn't raise the alarm looks suspicious," he said.

"I told you, I panicked," she shot back. "I knew how bad it would look if people found out what we'd been planning, so I kept my mouth shut and hoped I could get to the bottom of it myself. That's why I had Tonino take the meals to the guest room." Her gaze shifted to Anwen and Cerys. "Then you two arrived, and I realized the truth."

Anwen searched Flavia's face for any hint of deception, but found none. "Why would the Maestro kill Thibault?" she asked.

Flavia shook her head, and the glimmer of tears reappeared. "I don't know. They never liked each other, but the Maestro isn't a violent man."

"Apparently he is," said the Captain. "We could have been combing the city for him all this time. Instead, you've given him a two-day head start."

"I'm sorry, Captain. And Tonino, I deeply regret making you a part of this. You deserved better."

Tonino blushed furiously, and said nothing.

"Now, if you'll allow me a question of my own," said Flavia. "What exactly is wrong with the Chamberlain?"

At the mention of his title, the Chamberlain finally woke with a jolt. He looked around in consternation, and wiped a string of drool from his beard.

"He hasn't been well," said Anwen.

"Rubbish!" said the Chamberlain. "'m fine. Jus' restin' my eyes." He struggled free of the Captain and Marcus, but swayed so badly they had to grab him again before he fell.

"See that you make an appointment with the royal physicians," said Flavia. "The kingdom will need you at your best for as long as I'm gone."

The Chamberlain struggled to focus. "Gone, Your Majesty?"

Flavia nodded solemnly and got to her feet. "I'm ready, Captain."

The Captain composed himself. "Your Majesty. I'm arresting you for aiding and abetting the murder of King Thibault, and for obstructing the course of justice. Do you have anything to say?"

The whole room seemed to hold its breath.

"I've stated my case," said Flavia. "Let a court of law decide my fate."

The Captain motioned to two of the guards. After a moment's hesitation, they took up positions on either side of Flavia.

"Take her to her chambers," he told them. "And seal up the laundry chute in her room, just in case."

The volume of scandalized chatter swelled as the guards led Flavia away, her head held high.

"I never thought I'd say this," said Cerys. "But you did it. You solved the murder."

Anwen wanted to feel satisfied, maybe even smug, but she just felt strangely empty. Even though they had identified the killer, they were still a long way from catching him. Plus, there was still a question nagging at her—*why* had the Maestro done it? As the throne room doors closed behind Flavia, Anwen couldn't help thinking that she had missed something vital.

22
The Only Way Is Down

The sun had barely risen when Tonino carried Anwen and Cerys out to the piazza the next morning. The crowds of mourners were gone, replaced by the coils of a huge rope ladder, which wound around the square like a monstrous snake. A contingent of palace guards stood around the pit where the monument had once been, but there was no one else in sight.

Anwen reached up to pet Colin, who was perched on her shoulder. "Where is everyone?" she asked.

"It wouldn't kill them to give us a bit of a send-off," said Cerys, giving the bird a hateful look. Colin gave her one right back.

"I don't even know who's in charge anymore," said Tonino.

The words had barely left his mouth before a trumpet blast came from the palace, the gates swung open, and a procession appeared. Anwen recognized several of the court officials, and the Captain, but the thing that drew her eye was the golden sedan chair following behind them, carried on the shoulders of four burly footmen. Sitting atop the chair, in fur-lined purple robes, was the Chamberlain.

"Make way for the Lord Protector," announced one of the officials, and the guards all snapped to attention.

"Lord what?" said Tonino.

The Captain drew Tonino aside as the procession came to a stop in front of the pit. "There have been some changes," he said.

"Good changes?" asked Cerys.

"That depends on him," the Captain whispered, nodding to the Chamberlain as the footmen lowered the sedan chair and helped him alight.

"I'm busy, so let's keep this brief," said the Chamberlain.

An anxious lump formed in Anwen's stomach. "*You're* in charge?"

"Protocol dictates that I take on all Her Majesty's royal duties as long as she is . . . indisposed," he replied. "Which means I've got a funeral and a trial to organize before sundown." He massaged his temple with his fingertips. "Who has the basket?"

One of the servants produced a large wicker basket. It was the sort of thing Anwen sometimes used for shopping at Old Stump's market, with a thick handle looped over the top. It was lined with quilted velvet, and could easily have held ten full-grown cows.

"At least it's more comfortable than a beanstalk," said Cerys.

"Don't keep us all waiting, page boy," said the Chamberlain.

Tonino gently placed the girls in the basket. "It was wonderful knowing you," he said. "Thanks for everything."

Anwen felt that she would burst, she had so much she wanted to say to him, but a team of workmen had already surrounded them. They carried the bottommost rungs of the rope ladder between them, and one of their number—a broad-shouldered man covered in tattoos—tied a spare length of rope around the basket's handle. With deft fingers, he secured the other end around the bottom rung of the ladder.

"Wait," said the Captain. "Before you go, I want you to have this." He pulled a bulging silk purse, twice as tall as Anwen, from inside his breastplate. "It's not much, but it might help rebuild your village."

Cerys's eyes lit up. "Is that gold?"

Anwen silenced her with a nudge. "Thank you, Captain," she said. "You have no idea what a difference this will make."

"It's the least I can do," he replied, placing the purse between them in the basket. "I'd still be searching the city for Thibault if you hadn't arrived to help us. And I might never have gotten to the bottom of Professor Umberto's disappearance."

"And I'd still be helping Flavia cover it all up, without even realizing it," said Tonino.

"Touching," said the Chamberlain. "Now get them out of here, cover over this thin place, and find me the Maestro. I want him clapped in irons at Her Majesty's trial."

He retook his seat in the sedan chair, and snapped his fingers impatiently until the footmen hoisted him back onto their shoulders. Then, without a backward glance, his procession made its way back to the palace.

"There's someone I'm not going to miss," said Cerys.

"But we'll definitely miss you two," added Anwen. "I wish this wasn't goodbye."

"Me too," said Tonino. "I'd love to visit your world, and see more magic in action."

The tattooed workman, who was still holding the basket, cleared his throat impatiently.

The Captain nodded sadly. "Lower away."

Anwen and Cerys waved as the workman lowered

the rope with the basket attached, hand over hand, into the pit. Anwen's last view of Tonino and the Captain dissolved into tears a second before darkness enveloped them.

23

You Can't Go Home Again

One moment, Anwen and Cerys were in the depths of the hole in the piazza, the wicker basket hemmed in by rough dirt and old stone. Then, in an instant, they were through the thin place and dangling three thousand feet in the air above Old Stump.

Anwen wiped the tears from her eyes and saw the rope ladder trailing above them, appearing to vanish in midair where it entered the invisible hole between worlds. It didn't help her feel terribly secure, especially when the wind made the basket swing.

"Hold on!" she said.

"What do you think I'm doing?" Cerys replied.

Anwen's thoughts felt as turbulent as the basket—their investigation had come to an end so quickly, and she was still struggling to come to terms with it.

At last the wind abated, and the basket stilled.

"This feels all wrong," she said. "Don't you think?"

"Of course," said Cerys. "The palace could have afforded something nicer than an old basket. The Chamberlain put us in this to spite us."

"That's not what I meant," said Anwen. "We left without all the answers."

"Maybe it was impossible to find them all," said Cerys. "At least we got the big picture right."

"Did we, though?" said Anwen. "Was Thibault really faking his music? Why did the Maestro decide to kill him? And why did he drop Thibault's body on Old Stump?"

"That's the Captain's problem now," Cerys replied. "We did our part."

"I suppose so," said Anwen, but she didn't really mean it. The realization that she would never know the whole truth was almost painful.

As the basket descended, they plucked up the courage to look over the side. They were already close enough to wave at the small group of people assembling in the field beside Thibault's body. A minute later, the basket settled on the grass, and Anwen jumped out, straight into the waiting arms of Eira. Meredith joined them, wiping a tear from her eye, and Stillpike struck up a celebratory tune on his guitar.

"Welcome back, my dear," said Eira. "We got your note. It sounds like you had quite a time."

"I've got so much to tell you," said Anwen.

Beside her, Cerys embraced her parents, who were sobbing with relief.

"We thought we'd lost you!" her father said. "But look at you! You're dressed like a queen!"

"It's just a little something I threw on," she replied, pirouetting so that the gold sequined tails of her suit flared out behind her. "And wait until you see what we brought back. Open that big purse, Dad." She and Anwen grinned at each other as her father climbed into the basket, untied the neck of the purse, and looked inside. For a moment, he seemed too overcome to speak.

"Gold," he said, in a tiny voice. Then, louder, "It's gold! A whole bank vault's worth!"

Stillpike's music stopped abruptly. "We're rich!" he cried. "Well done, girls. It wasn't a wasted trip."

"It's not for us," said Anwen. "It's to rebuild the village."

Stillpike's face fell. "Oh. A noble cause, to be sure. But perhaps if there's any left over . . ."

"Left over?" Mr. Powell laughed. Then, grunting with effort, he lifted out a coin almost two feet in diameter. "There's enough in here to build twenty villages!"

Anwen gasped. "I had no idea it was so much."

"A fortune for each of us," said Stillpike. "Why rebuild a cottage when you can have a mansion?"

"There will be no mansions, thank you," said

Eira. "We'll use whatever's necessary to rebuild Old Stump, and keep the rest in trust."

Stillpike looked incredulous. "Why?"

"You never know when there's going to be a bad harvest, or winter floods," said Eira. "This will give us something to fall back on when times are hard. Now let's clear the area. The giants will be here for the body soon, and I want to give them room."

"And we need to get you to Oldport, my darling," said Cerys's mother. "Maybe it's not too late to find you another coach leaving for the capital."

Cerys's smile was almost as dazzling as her suit. "Yes, please!"

The group made for the field hospital. As they walked, Anwen caught Cerys by the arm and drew her discreetly to one side.

"That's it?" she asked. "You're leaving?"

"I know it's sudden, but what else am I supposed to do?" said Cerys.

"You could at least say goodbye," Anwen replied. "And help me explain to everyone what we've been doing."

"You don't need me for that," said Cerys. "If I leave now, I can reach Oldport by lunchtime."

"Oh good," said Anwen. "You're thinking about lunch already."

She regretted the words as soon as she'd said them, but didn't have time to apologize before Cerys rounded on her.

"Do you want to know why I've been eating so much?" she asked. "It's because I'm starving. Literally."

"What do you mean?" said Anwen.

"You've got all the pieces in front of you, but you still don't get it. Remember what you told Tonino? High Magic is for rich people."

"So?"

Cerys gestured to her parents, who, along with the others, were now out of earshot. "My parents are pig farmers, Anwen. It's costing them everything to send me to the Academy. None of us have eaten a proper meal for months. I use glamour dresses because I've got nothing but rags left." Her eyes shone with repressed tears. "I almost turned down my place, but Mum and Dad insisted I go. They've worked so hard for it. I can't let them down now."

Anwen's stomach dropped, as she realized that Cerys was right—she'd failed to recognize what was right in front of her all along. "I had no idea."

"Of course you didn't," said Cerys. "Because you're so obsessed with proving that you're better than me. Admit it, you never thought I really deserved my place at the Academy."

"I . . ." Anwen faltered. She wanted to lie, but knew that Cerys would see straight through it. "I'm sorry," she said at last.

"So am I," said Cerys, the tears starting to fall. "Because I was really starting to like you. But now I don't think I'll miss you at all."

She turned and ran, leaving Anwen to nurse her guilt.

If I couldn't figure that out, no wonder I wasn't able to solve Thibault's murder properly, she thought. *And now it's too late.* She was about to start after Cerys when Stillpike cried out.

"What's that?"

Several giants were descending the rope ladder. Anwen recognized the tattooed workman and three of his colleagues.

"The invasion!" Stillpike cried. "It's started!"

"Don't be silly," Eira chided. "They're here to collect the body."

"That's what they want us to think," Stillpike replied. "I'm not sticking around to get trodden on. It's everyone for themselves!" He slung his guitar over his back and sprinted away as the giants touched down in the field. They looked around, clearly as amazed by the sight of this strange new world as Anwen and Cerys had been by the Sky Kingdom.

"Sorry for the intrusion," said the man with the tattoos. "We won't be long."

The four giants quickly wrapped Thibault's body in a thick golden sheet, then slung it like an enormous hammock from the bottom of the ladder. They began climbing back up, and the ladder itself slowly rose into the sky. As Thibault's body lifted clear of the ground, it revealed the pulverized remains of Old Stump for the first time. Thibault's weight had ground the buildings into dust.

Eira watched them go. "Whatever else might have happened, I'm quite glad I got to see this," she said. "Aren't you?" When Anwen didn't respond, Eira looked around but couldn't find her. "Where are you, dear?"

A flurry of motion caught her attention—Cerys was fending off Colin the seagull, who was trying to perch on her head.

"Anwen!" Cerys cried. "Is this some sort of revenge attack? Get him off!"

Colin cawed, and Eira's brow furrowed.

"He says Anwen will make it up to you when she gets back from . . ." She blanched. "From getting her answers."

Cerys shooed Colin away and looked at the rising group of giants. "Oh no," she said. "Look."

Eira followed her pointing finger and saw the tiny speck of green clinging to one of the ropes carrying Thibault's body. The speck of green waved to them.

"That girl is incorrigible," said Eira.

"I can't think where she gets it from," said Meredith. Eira scowled at her.

"What are we going to do?" asked Cerys. "We can't just let her go up there alone. They're going to close the thin place later today. What if she gets trapped up there forever?"

24

The Music Man

The ride back up to the thin place was slow and painful. The wind threatened to pluck Anwen off the rope and fling her into the sky. She dug her fingers even deeper into the fibers and tensed every muscle. Her decision to return to the Sky Kingdom suddenly felt very foolish, and she envied Cerys for staying behind. Nevertheless, a small, quiet voice inside her whispered that she was doing the right thing—her investigation was unfinished. She still had a duty to the dead.

At last, the ropes hauled Thibault's body up through the thin place and out of the hole in the piazza. The body was lowered onto an ornate golden bier, and nobody saw Anwen as she let go of the rope and fell into the pile of flowers that surrounded the bier on all sides. She landed on a scarlet dahlia, as soft as a pillow, and rolled off into a cluster of carnations.

She shimmied down the stems to the ground, and peeked out from behind the petals. The ropes were already being cleared away, and mourners flocked from all directions, eager to see their former king lying in state.

Anwen had helped Eira dress plenty of bodies for similar viewings over the years—it was a chance for people to say their goodbyes and pay their respects.

But it presented her with a challenge, as hundreds of pairs of giant feet tramped toward the bier. She would have to find her way through them, and back into the palace, if she was going to get anything done. Trying it on foot was clearly going to get her squashed, so she looked at the sky. A few birds circled high above, but it took her a moment to spot the one she wanted—a speck of gray and iridescent green, perched on the palace roof. Archimboldo.

How was she going to attract his attention from all the way down here? Even with the amplification spell, he was too far away to hear her. It was then that she heard a contented buzzing from behind her, and turned to see a chubby bumblebee dipping its legs into the pollen of a vivid purple gladiolus.

"Excuse me, Mr. Bee," she said. The bee raised its antennae toward her in polite curiosity, and Anwen fought to remember the various gestures and dances needed to properly communicate with bees. "Would you mind . . ." she said, hopping from foot to foot, ". . . flying up to the palace . . ." She spun around and waggled her bottom. ". . . and asking that pigeon to fly down here, please?" She finished with a star jump, windmilling her arms.

The bee buzzed and hummed in reply, stroking its wings and bobbing back and forth.

"Yes, I know I'm not very fluent, but it's difficult to speak insect when you don't have six limbs," she said. "Just please go and ask him. He's a friend of mine."

The bee took off with bad grace, buzzing on about tourists never bothering to learn the language properly, and Anwen thought it might have ignored her request altogether. But a minute later, a shining gray-and-turquoise head pushed its way into the flowers, and the large orange eye of Archimboldo fixed on her.

"Am I glad to see you!" said Anwen, throwing her arms around his neck. "I'll explain everything on the way, but we need to find Tonino."

The nursery window was shut, as was Thibault's, so Archimboldo flapped up to the roof and landed in the shadow of a chimney. A nearby tile had come loose, revealing a sliver of darkness beneath, and Anwen slipped off his back and hurried toward it.

"This is perfect," she said. "You can teach me a whole course on art history for this."

Archimboldo clearly liked this idea, and fluffed out his chest with pride.

"Wait here," she said. "I'll be back."

She could make out a rough wooden beam just below the gap in the tile, so she wriggled through and dropped onto it. She was in the palace attic, and it felt strangely like the barns and farmhouses back home. She closed her eyes and drank in the smell of warm dust, listened to the distant rustle of sleeping bats, and, sure enough, the patter of mice going about their business.

When she opened her eyes, however, she couldn't see them. The attic was dark, and filled with old junk, crammed haphazardly into whatever corner was available. Some of it looked very old indeed, but it offered her an easy way down to the ground.

"Hello?" she called when she reached the uneven floorboards. "It's me, Anwen. I'm looking for the palace mischief. Can you hear me?"

She held her breath and listened, but no response came. The skittering had stopped, or moved away to another part of the attic.

She set off, hoping to find some other sign of the mice, until she rounded the base of an enormous vase and stopped in her tracks. Before her, bathed in a shaft of light from a small window high above, was a mansion with a gilded roof, bay windows, and wrought iron balconies. It sat alone in the middle of the floor, and, unlike the other contents of the attic, it was spotlessly clean. The words FAME HALL were written in gold script above the door.

"Thibault's old dollhouse," she said. "But what's it doing here?"

An answering squeak came from behind her, and she turned to see Garibaldi, the leader of the mischief's mouse scouts, emerge from behind a bucket full of old umbrellas.

"Hello again!" She got down on one knee, and he approached her eagerly. "I hope the palace cats haven't been any trouble."

The mouse put a paw on her arm and gave a reassuring squeak.

"I'm glad," she said. "But I need another favor. I'm looking for my friend Tonino."

Instead of answering, Garibaldi suddenly reared up on his hind legs, his great ears swiveling side to side.

"What's wrong?" whispered Anwen, looking around in alarm. Visions of cats loomed large in her imagination.

Then she heard it herself—the floorboards groaned as something behind the nearest stack of junk shifted its weight. It sounded too heavy for a cat, but not too heavy for a giant.

Someone's here!

Her skin prickled with fear, and she followed Garibaldi in a crouching run to the cover of the bucket. There was just room, between it and an antique armchair, for them to squeeze through and peer nervously out the other side.

"I don't see anyone," she whispered.

They had found a part of the attic devoted to storing clothes. Towering wardrobes overflowed with moth-eaten dresses, suits, and uniforms—so many that they spilled out onto the floor. A row of giant mannequins stood opposite, their painted wooden faces blank and expressionless. The whole scene gave Anwen the creeps.

She stole out from cover, senses alert to any sounds, but Garibaldi refused to follow. "Come on," she whispered. "I think we're safe. Let's find Tonino."

Garibaldi gave an almost inaudible squeak in response.

"Footprints?" Only then did she look down and realize her mistake.

The dust covering the floorboards had been disturbed, and she was standing in the middle of a giant shoeprint. It was one of several cutting a trail across the floor. A trail that led straight to the nearest mannequin.

Her breath turned to ice in her throat. With mounting dread, she raised her eyes from the figure's feet to its face. It blinked.

Anwen screamed and fled toward Garibaldi, but the giant covered the space between them with one stride.

"Stop!" he cried, bringing a foot down to block her path. The floor bucked, throwing her onto her back. She scrambled upright and ran in the other direction, only for the giant to stamp his boot down again.

"Garibaldi!" she cried. "Help!"

The little mouse was at her side in a blur of brown fur. She threw herself at him, but before he could carry her to safety, the giant let out a piercing shriek and leapt into the air. He crashed backward into the row of mannequins, which toppled like enormous dominoes. Within seconds, he was trapped in a tangle of wooden limbs and trailing clothes.

"Keep it away from me!" he wailed.

Garibaldi nudged Anwen, urging her to run, but she put a steadying hand between his ears. "Wait," she said.

The giant was staring at Garibaldi with a look of absolute terror. He seemed paralyzed with fear.

She quickly activated her amplification spell. "Musophobia," she said. "You have a fear of rodents."

The giant nodded frantically. He was old and portly, with a blotchy red wine tint to his features. He wore an ill-fitting and badly stained butler's uniform, but what drew Anwen's eye was the wink of gold at his left wrist. The cuffs of his shirtsleeves protruded from the uniform coat—the right cuff flapped open, but the left was held shut with a gold-and-white cuff link in the shape of a musical clef.

"You're the Maestro!" she exclaimed. "So *this* is where you've been hiding?"

"I confess!" he said. "Just, please, don't let it come any closer!"

Anwen stroked Garibaldi's head, and a new sense of determination took hold of her. "You confess to King Thibault's murder?"

The words punched through the Maestro's terror. "What? No! Of course not."

"But you just said—"

"I confess that I'm the Maestro," he replied. "I never laid a finger on Thibault."

Anwen's determination slipped a little. "But you're the most wanted man in the kingdom," she said. "Flavia confessed everything. We know she invited you to Thibault's concert to discredit him. You were only supposed to watch him play the guitar, and see if it was enchanted, but you killed him. Was it jealousy?

A fit of rage? And why did you dump his body into my world?"

The Maestro was sweating heavily now. "I don't know what you're talking about."

"Oh really?" she replied. "Show me your head."

Trying to keep his eyes on Garibaldi, the Maestro slowly inclined his head, revealing an ugly purple welt on his scalp.

"I knew it," said Anwen. "There were two bloodstains on the bust that killed Thibault. You and he fought, and he injured you."

"You're wrong," said the Maestro. "I was in Thibault's room, but I never saw him after I left the banquet. I didn't even get to examine the guitar."

Anwen hesitated. He sounded too scared to be insincere. "Why not?" she asked.

"Because someone tried to kill me before I got the chance," he replied.

25

The Concert That Wasn't

A long, dusty silence filled the attic as Anwen tried to make sense of what the Maestro had just said.

"Someone attacked you?" she asked.

"Almost the moment I stepped into Thibault's room," he replied, keeping a nervous eye on Garibaldi. "I had a research book with me, *A History of Magical Music*, and made straight for the guitar for an initial inspection. The guitar's the key to the whole thing, you see. But I'd barely set eyes on it before someone crept up behind me and smashed me over the head. I went flying into the bookcase and lost consciousness." He put a hand to the lump on his skull and winced. "They must have assumed they'd killed me, because when I regained my senses, more than an hour later, I was in the laundry room, wrapped in a bloodied bedsheet, alongside Thibault." The Maestro shut his eyes and grimaced. "He was already dead. A blow to the head, just like mine. I'm certain the same attacker was responsible."

"Who?" asked Anwen. "Do you have any idea?"

"None," said the Maestro. "But I know who must have sent them. Flavia! She was the only person who knew where I was."

"But she thinks *you* killed Thibault," said Anwen.

"A likely story," the Maestro replied. "I've had two days to think it all through. With me out of the way, Flavia could blame the mysterious Professor Umberto for the whole affair. And if it finally surfaced that the Professor and I were one and the same, why, who better to take the blame? Half the kingdom knows about my falling out with Thibault."

Anwen couldn't deny that this theory made sense, and it made all her previous certainties feel suddenly fragile. Had she been wrong all this time?

"What did you do when you woke up in the laundry room?" she asked.

"I fled, of course, before Flavia's assassin realized I wasn't dead. I stole this uniform from the dirty laundry pile as a disguise, and crept up here while the rest of the staff were outside at the concert. I didn't dare flee the palace with so many people in the piazza. Someone might have recognized me. I've tried to sneak out since, but there are guards everywhere. I'm stuck here, and let me tell you, it's not much of a life."

"Wait a minute," said Anwen. "The concert was still going on when you left the laundry room?"

"That's right," said the Maestro. "I passed a clock in one of the hallways. It was about ten past eleven."

"But you said that Thibault was already dead when you woke up," she said. "How could he be dead in the laundry room and performing on his balcony at the same time?"

A humorless smile spread across the Maestro's lips. "I don't think he ever was performing, on his balcony or anywhere else. The guitar was doing it all for him. Or rather, someone else was doing it all for him, and using the guitar as a conduit."

"How?" asked Anwen.

"With magic, of course," the Maestro replied. "And before you give me any tedious guff about giants not being able to use magic, you're right. That's the part I didn't understand, and why I wanted to see the whole charade in action, close up."

Anwen felt as if the puzzle she had carefully assembled over the last two days had just been tossed up in the air and all the pieces were raining down around her. "If Thibault wasn't actually performing," she said, thinking aloud, "then he really could have been dead before the end of the concert." She remembered something Tonino had told her, and gasped. "Thibault went inside when it got cold! The crowd could hear him, but they couldn't see him."

"They heard the real performer," said the Maestro. "Playing through the enchanted guitar, like a ventriloquist throwing his voice."

Anwen began rearranging the pieces of evidence. "The killer must have been hiding in Thibault's room before you got there," she said. "You surprised them when you snuck in, and they attacked you. But their real target was Thibault, so they hid you somewhere out of sight, then went back into hiding and waited for Thibault to begin the concert."

She fussed with the strand of hair where her heather should have been. "They needed the public to see him out on the balcony," she said. "If the concert hadn't gone ahead, everyone would have realized that something was wrong. So they let him play the first half, and killed him when he came in off the balcony to get warm. The guitar kept on playing and singing by itself, and nobody outside on the piazza noticed the difference."

The Maestro's curiosity seemed to be overcoming his fear. "I have no idea who you are, or what you're doing in our world, but you're clearly a very bright girl," he said. "Perhaps you'd be so good as to help me clear my name?"

"Gladly," she replied. "But we need proof. Your book, *A History of Magical Music*—where is it?"

"I was holding it when I was attacked. Either

the killer took it with them, or it's still in Thibault's room."

"We have to get back in there and check. Garibaldi? Time to go."

The mouse squeaked in agreement, and she climbed onto his back.

"How remarkable," said the Maestro. "Is this what magic looks like in action?"

"It is when I do it," said Anwen. "Stay here. If everything goes well, I'll send someone up to help you."

"What are you going to do?" he said.

Anwen smiled at him. "Find your book, find out the truth about Thibault's guitar, and find the real killer."

26
A Book of Revelations

Anwen and Garibaldi emerged from the mouse runs beneath the large wardrobe in Thibault's bedroom.

"The mischief really does get everywhere," she said, giving the mouse an affectionate pat as she climbed off him and looked around. As she had hoped, the room was deserted.

"The Maestro was holding his book when he was attacked," she said. "And he fell into the bookcase before he blacked out."

All the titles on the bookcase beside the wardrobe were neatly shelved. Not a thing looked out of place.

"We're looking for a book that doesn't fit," she said, turning in a slow circle. Like a magnet dragging a compass needle, her thoughts drew her to the bedside table, where she could see the corner of the book on crop rotation sticking out over the side. "That's been bothering me ever since I saw it," she said. "Why would Thibault ever read a book like that? It doesn't belong there."

Garibaldi gave a squeak of polite interest, and paused to wash his whiskers. Anwen knew he wasn't really following the conversation, but it helped her to think out loud.

She turned back to the bookcase.

"But of course, *none* of these books really belong here," she continued. "Thibault never read any of them. The whole bookcase is just for decoration. So why did he have a book by his bed?"

She closed her eyes and pictured the Maestro facing the guitar stand; the shadowy figure of Thibault's killer sneaking up behind him; the blow to the head, the reeling crash into the bookcase; his copy of *A History of Magical Music* slipping from his fingers . . .

She opened her eyes wide. "The crop rotation book wasn't on the bedside table when the Maestro was attacked," she said. "It was here, in the bookcase, with all the others, until the Maestro bumped into it. He dropped his own book, and dislodged a load of the others. Crash!" She threw her arms up. "They all came tumbling out, and the killer was left with one unconscious Maestro, and a mess of books all over the floor. They hid the Maestro out of sight somewhere, and tidied the books back onto the shelves. But now there was one extra, and they wouldn't all fit. The killer didn't have time to think about it, so they put the extra book on the bedside table, where they thought it wouldn't look out of place, which means . . ." She swung back to the bookcase. "The killer put the Maestro's book back on the shelves without realizing it."

She started reading the spines of the books and, sure enough, on the third shelf from the bottom, she found it: *A History of Magical Music*.

"I finally figured it out!" she cried, hugging Garibaldi with excitement. "Now I just have to get it down."

But how? The shelf was almost thirty feet above her, and the book looked heavy. She was still searching for an answer when she heard footsteps approaching the bedroom door.

"I want that guitar spotless and shining before we take it anywhere near the public" came the Chamberlain's voice. "They need to see it in Thibault's hands one last time before the funeral."

Garibaldi bolted for cover beneath the bed, but Anwen was caught in the open as the Chamberlain strode in. She panicked, until she saw that he was flanked on one side by Marcus, and on the other by . . .

"Tonino!"

Her voice was still amplified following her conversation with the Maestro, and Tonino's face lit up in a huge smile.

"Anwen!" He stooped and picked her up in his cupped hands. "I thought I'd never see you again."

The Chamberlain bared his teeth. "What the devil are you doing here?"

"Solving the murder," she replied. "Where's the Captain?"

"He's out hunting for the Maestro," said Marcus. "Why, have you found something?"

"I've found the Maestro, and he's not the killer," Anwen replied. "There was someone else in here on the night of the concert, and it's all connected to Thibault's guitar. I'm here to prove it."

"Nonsense," said the Chamberlain. "Page boy, this creature no longer has any guest privileges in this palace. Deliver her to the nearest guard and have her locked up immediately."

Tonino held Anwen to his chest. "If Anwen says she has answers, we should listen."

"I agree," said Marcus, putting himself between them and the Chamberlain.

Anwen wished she could have hugged them both, if only her arms were big enough.

"I should have you *all* locked up," said the Chamberlain. "This is treason!"

Looking at the Chamberlain's reddening face and wild eyes, Anwen felt a horrible new suspicion growing in her. Who had really benefited most from Thibault's murder? Certainly not Flavia. "It was you," she said.

"What?" rasped the Chamberlain.

"Cerys was right all along," she replied. "You weren't just ill, you used it as a cover so you could sneak around without being suspected. You were the other person hiding in this room that night. *You* killed Thibault."

The Chamberlain went pale. "Preposterous."

"Were you going to kill Flavia next?" she asked. "Or did you plan for her to share the blame with the Maestro and give up the throne? Either way, it leaves you in charge."

"Do you think I want any of this?" the Chamberlain spluttered. "None of this responsibility is supposed to be mine."

"Let's all calm down for a moment," said Marcus. "Anwen, tell us everything, please, starting with the Maestro. Where is he?"

"Up in the attic, trying to escape from a pile of dummies," she said. "If what he says is true, Thibault really was a fake. Somebody else was playing the guitar and singing for him all along, and that book over there can prove it." She pointed, and Tonino pulled *A History of Magical Music* off the shelf.

He lifted her onto his shoulder, to give her a clear view as he leafed quickly through the old, brittle pages.

"Talking harps . . ." said Tonino, reading aloud. "Flutes for hypnotizing rats and disobedient children . . . An enchanted cowbell that controls the weather . . ." He jabbed a finger down at an entry. "The mimic guitar. Could this be it?"

"I don't know who Thibault's accomplice was," said Anwen, "but this should tell us how they got the magic to work. It might give us some new leads to follow."

"Then we should get it to Cato," said Marcus. He extended a hand, and Tonino passed the book over.

"Excuse me!" said the Chamberlain. "Need I remind you that I'm the one in charge here? I'll decide what happens."

"I've got a better idea," said Marcus. He tucked the book inside his tunic, crossed to the shelves beside the wardrobe, and picked up the golden bust. It still bore the two bloodstains from the night of the murder.

"What are you doing?" the Chamberlain demanded. "Put that back."

Marcus weighed the bust carefully in his hands.

Then, before anyone could react, he brought it crashing down on the Chamberlain's head. Anwen screamed and closed her eyes, but not before she saw the Chamberlain crumple to the floor.

27

With Friends Like These

Tonino leapt backward in shock, almost tipping Anwen off his shoulder as he bumped into the wardrobe.

"What have you done?" he cried.

Anwen opened her eyes to see Marcus standing over the crumpled form of the Chamberlain, and felt as if she had plunged through a sheet of ice into freezing waters. "*You* killed Thibault?" she gasped.

"He had it coming," said Marcus. "Although this was never really about him. It's about the guitar."

Anwen fought down a wave of revulsion. "But why? I thought you could already play."

Marcus's face reddened. "You don't know what it feels like to have your lifelong dream torn to shreds," he said. "To be told you're not good enough."

The unwelcome memory of her Academy entrance exam instantly resurfaced, along with all the feelings of shame and inadequacy that came with it. "Maybe I do," she said. Marcus hefted the bust again, and she knew she had to keep him talking if she wanted to stop him using it. "You told me that you and the

Captain wanted to be a superstar musicians," she said. "Is that what all this is about?"

Marcus's face crumpled into a look of hatred. "Cato and me, we could've been great. And we would've been, if the Maestro had only given us the chance."

The connection sparked in Anwen's mind like lightning jumping between clouds. "Your audition at the School of the Arts," she said. "Was he the judge?"

Marcus nodded. "We worked so hard, and he just turned us away. Cato gave up, but I knew there had to be another way of hitting the big time. And then Thibault happened." He turned the bust until he was looking it in the face. "This idiot couldn't play a note, and he suddenly became the world's greatest guitarist. For once, I agreed with the Maestro—it couldn't be natural talent. So I started watching Thibault closely. It was easy to get a master key—the Chamberlain makes me polish all his keys once a week. Another ridiculous bit of palace protocol." He laughed. "I started letting myself in here to investigate whenever Thibault wasn't around."

"Exactly what the Maestro was planning," said Anwen.

"He had the right idea," Marcus replied. "But I learned the truth months ago. Thibault had a partner. And now they're *my* partner."

A burning curiosity eclipsed Anwen's fear for a moment. "Who?"

He opened his mouth to respond, then closed it again. "You already know too much," he said. "I'm sorry." He advanced on them. Tonino tried retreating farther, but his back was already against the wardrobe doors.

"You'll never get away with this," said Tonino. "You can't cover up three more murders!"

Marcus paused. "I'll deal with the Maestro, and blame it all on him." He raised the bust above his head and was about to bring it smashing down on Tonino when a single, clear note rang out from the guitar.

Marcus froze. "Already?" He turned to the instrument, and the note sounded again. Anwen saw one of the strings trembling, as if plucked by an invisible finger. Marcus was trembling now too.

"At last!" he said. "My public debut!"

It wasn't much of a distraction, but Anwen knew it was their only chance.

"Run!" she shouted.

Tonino made a break for the door, but Marcus moved to block him. He raised the bust again, but Tonino had already turned and opened the wardrobe door. He jumped in, Anwen clinging to his ear, and pulled the door shut behind them a second before the bust smashed against the wood. The wardrobe shook, but the door held.

"Come out!" Marcus bellowed. The door rattled as he tried to pull it open, but Tonino took hold of a clothes hook mounted on the inside and pulled back.

Marcus delivered another blow with the bust, but was interrupted by the guitar, which sounded the same urgent note, three times in quick succession. Marcus cursed under his breath. "I'll deal with you soon," he said. "The whole city's gathered outside to mourn their king. They're the perfect audience."

Anwen heard furniture scraping across the floor, then something heavy bumped against the wardrobe.

She and Tonino held their breath as they listened to Marcus's footsteps retreat across the room to the balcony.

"Ladies and gentlemen!" they heard him cry. "We're here to remember a great man. He was a hero to all of us, but, to me, he was also a friend."

From outside, the faint murmur of the crowd fell silent.

"I can't believe this," said Tonino. "He bought me a toffee apple, and now he's going to kill us!"

"Focus," Anwen replied. "We need to get out of here."

Tonino tried the door, but it refused to budge. "He's blocked it with something."

Meanwhile, Marcus continued to address the crowd. "Because I was his friend, I helped King Thibault keep a life-changing secret from the world. You see, he didn't really teach himself to play this guitar." He paused, and Anwen could make out the expectant silence from the crowd. "I taught him!" The crowd erupted in consternation.

At the same time, the wardrobe door finally yielded a couple of inches. At least, a couple of inches in giant terms.

"I can get through that," said Anwen. "Put me down."

Tonino obeyed, and she squeezed through and dropped to the carpet below. She landed beside a clothes chest, which had been dragged across the wardrobe doors.

"There's no way I can move this," she said, looking up at the sliver of Tonino's face visible through the gap. "I'll have to get help."

"Who?" said Tonino. "Almost everyone's outside."

Anwen's mind whirled. "The Maestro. He's our best hope. Garibaldi?"

The mouse appeared from beneath the wardrobe, whiskers twitching.

"Thank goodness you're still here! I need to get back to the attic, quickly."

She was swinging her leg over the mouse's flank when Marcus cried, "This is in memory of our friend, Thibault!" and launched into his first song. It was a mournful love ballad about a lost sweetheart, and it rooted her to the spot.

"I know this song," she replied.

"Everyone does," said Tonino. "It was one of Thibault's biggest hits. Now hurry up and get me out of here!"

But Anwen couldn't bring herself to move. It was as if the music was holding her in place. "I never heard Thibault play," she said. "But that sounds exactly like . . ."

Then Marcus started singing, and she knew for certain.

"That voice . . ." she said. "That's Stillpike!"

28
Swan Song

The Maestro was setting the last of the dummies back on its feet when Garibaldi shot out from a nearby pile of junk and deposited Anwen in front of him. He gave a piercing shriek, and almost fell backward into the wooden figures again.

"Come quickly!" Anwen cried. "I've found your book, and the murderer, but he has my friend trapped. We need your help."

"Me?" The Maestro looked flustered. "But I'm a wanted man."

"I don't care," she replied. "A man called Marcus attacked you, and killed Thibault. He's going to kill my friend Tonino next if we don't do something to stop him."

With obvious effort, the Maestro tore his eyes away from Garibaldi and drew himself up.

"Very well," he said. "Tell me where to find this villain."

"He's on Thibault's balcony, serenading the crowd," she replied. "Tonino's trapped in the wardrobe in the bedroom."

"What if someone tries to stop me?"

"Make sure they don't," she replied. "Tonino will vouch for you once he's free, but you *have* to make it to Thibault's chambers. Please hurry! I'll get word to the Captain."

"You can count on me, young lady."

The Maestro hurried away into the maze of junk, churning up clouds of dust that forced Anwen to cover her mouth and nose. Even Garibaldi sneezed.

Before the dust could settle, a sound reached her through the gloom—the faint strains of a guitar. At first she thought it must be Marcus's performance, drifting up from the balcony, but there were no windows open and, most of all, the sound was too small. These weren't the chords of a giant guitar, but a human-sized one.

And it was coming from somewhere inside the attic.

"Wait here," she told Garibaldi, and let the music guide her. She squeezed past the rusty bucket full of umbrellas and emerged in front of Fame Hall, spotlighted by a shaft of light through the dirty window high above. The tune was clearer now, and it was another one she knew well—an old sailors' song called "Fflat Huw Puw." One of Stillpike's favorites.

A shiver of foreboding ran through her as she

realized that the tune was coming from inside the dollhouse.

Time to put a stop to this, she told herself.

The front door swung open at her touch, and the thick baize carpet softened her footsteps as she crept up the stairs to a pair of double doors. She pushed them wide and entered a lavish ballroom with a huge chandelier overhead. The dance floor was occupied by a troop of china dolls in ball gowns and suits, all posed as if frozen mid-waltz. In the center of it all, on a miniature replica of Flavia's golden throne, lounged Stillpike.

He looked up sharply as Anwen entered, but didn't stop playing. Instead, between strumming, he tapped the side of his guitar three times with his thumb.

"Stillpike." Anwen advanced until she stood in front of him. "You were behind everything, right from the start."

Stillpike brought the song to a close with a flourish. Then he twisted the fingers of his left hand into a complicated arrangement on the guitar's fretboard and picked out five notes in quick succession. Anwen felt the slightest crackle of magic jump from the air into the instrument before Stillpike set it down carefully.

"You're not supposed to be here, m'dear," he said, getting to his feet.

"Neither are you," she replied.

"That's where you're wrong. I'm exactly where I'm supposed to be, and it's taken a year's hard graft to get here."

"Hard graft?" said Anwen. "Is that what you call murder?"

He gave her a pained look. "Killing Thibault was unfortunate," he said. "But it had to be done."

"Why?"

"Because he made me a promise he wasn't willing to keep," Stillpike replied. "He had to be replaced."

"You mean you made a deal with him," said Anwen. "Your music in return for . . . what?"

"In return for all this." He spread his hands, indicating the mansion surrounding them. "A life of luxury, here in the Sky Kingdom."

This triggered so many questions that Anwen held her tongue while she sifted through them to find the most important.

"How did you strike a deal?" she asked. "It was impossible to contact the giants until Grandma planted her beanstalk."

"Not impossible for anyone with their hands on this little beauty," said Stillpike. He patted his guitar. "It's linked by magic to Thibault's. Anything I play or sing on this is reproduced exactly by the other."

"Even when they're in different worlds," she said.

Stillpike grinned. "You're a smart one, Anwen Sedge."

"How did you get it?"

"Pure luck," he replied. "I bought it from an old peddler who thought it was an ordinary instrument, but I grew up on stories of these guitars. It only took a little experimentation to prove what I'd gotten my hands on." He picked up the guitar and caressed it.

"A mimic guitar," said Anwen.

"It was crafted with High Magic, but all you need to use it is a bit of musical know-how," said Stillpike. "I had no way of knowing if its twin had survived up here in the Sky Kingdom, of course, until I woke the magic, tried a few songs, and suddenly heard a voice speaking back to me."

"Thibault."

"That's right." Stillpike laid the guitar carefully back across the throne's armrests. "He'd been shirking his responsibilities up here in the attic when my playing drew him to this guitar's twin. We talked, and I realized I had a remarkable opportunity on my hands."

"Don't tell me," said Anwen. "He was jealous that Flavia was due to inherit the throne, so you helped him change his father's mind by making him a star."

Stillpike smoothed down his mustache. "And thanks to my abundant talents, the whole scheme worked like a charm."

Anwen fought to wrap her head around the idea that the funny little man who mesmerized pixies for spare change in Old Stump market was secretly the most beloved musician in the Sky Kingdom. "Was this your reward?" she asked. "Being kept like a pet?"

"The happiest pet that ever lived!" Stillpike shot back. "Is that too much to ask, after forty years of scraping a living in pubs and market squares?"

Anwen had to admit that, while it was clearly dishonest, it sounded a lot better than murder. "You said Thibault broke his promise."

Stillpike scowled. "My ride to the Sky Kingdom never appeared," he replied. "It was always 'the wrong time' or 'too complicated.' I finally realized the selfish oaf had no intention of helping me."

"Why not stop playing for him?"

"And give up what I was owed?" said Stillpike. "I was lucky Marcus came along when he did."

Anwen remembered the sight of Marcus standing over the Chamberlain's body, and shuddered. "He discovered Thibault was a fraud," she said.

"Yes, he figured out the whole ruse pretty quickly," said Stillpike. "I thought the jig was up the first time he contacted me through the guitar. But he didn't want to expose us—he wanted me to give him the same fame I'd given Thibault."

The cold, sick feeling in Anwen's stomach grew. "Which meant that Thibault had to go."

"Hardly a great loss," Stillpike replied. "I did the planning, and Marcus got his hands dirty. That's a real partnership."

Despite her disgust, Anwen realized she finally had the last missing piece of the puzzle.

"You told Marcus to dump Thibault's body on Old Stump!" she cried. "You needed a way into the Sky Kingdom, and you knew a dead giant falling from the sky would force somebody to plant a beanstalk."

"Guilty as charged," said Stillpike. "Everyone within ten miles of Old Stump suspected your grandmother had that magic bean stashed away somewhere. And even if she didn't, the army would have come and planted one eventually."

Anwen's anger finally boiled over. "You destroyed the whole village!"

"For all the good it did," he said. "The blessed beanstalk crumbled into dust before I could get up it, so I ended up hitching a ride in one of Thibault's pockets. I suppose he finally made good on his promise after all."

Anwen wrinkled her nose in disgust. "People are hurt and homeless because of you."

"And I'd do it all again," said Stillpike. "I've finally gotten what I want."

"You haven't gotten anything," Anwen replied. "The Maestro's on his way to stop Marcus right now, and I'm going to tell everyone what you've done. You and Marcus are going to jail."

Stillpike's expression hardened. "I'm not going anywhere, missy." He shouldered past her to the nearest pair of dolls. The male doll wore a military dress uniform, complete with medals and an ornamental saber, which gave a whispering hiss as Stillpike pulled it from its scabbard.

Anwen's scalp crawled with fear. The blade looked as sharp as the real thing.

She turned to run, but lost her footing on the polished dance floor and crashed to the ground.

"I'm sorry, m'dear," said Stillpike, standing over her. "But if I have to choose between your future and mine, there's no contest."

He raised the saber, and the ballroom began to melt.

He and Anwen looked around in disbelief as the walls and ceiling ran like colored wax, dripping in long stalactites and pooling on the dance floor.

"What's this?" hissed Stillpike, the saber still raised. "Stop it!"

"I can't," said Anwen. "I'm not doing anything."

The molten strands of ballroom began to bubble and quickly dissolved into a thick cloud of steam that filled the whole room, obscuring everything.

The mist cleared as suddenly as it had formed, and Anwen saw that two things had changed. First, the ballroom was intact again. Second, she and Stillpike were now on the ceiling, the chandelier rising over them like a glittering tree. A wave of vertigo overcame her as she looked down on the dance floor, thirty feet below. Stillpike cried out in fear and confusion, dropped the saber, and threw himself at the chandelier, desperate for something to cling on to. To Anwen's astonishment, he passed straight through it as if he were a ghost.

Anwen was still trying to take it all in when a pair of hands grabbed her by the shoulders and dragged her to her feet. "Are you hurt?" Cerys asked.

Anwen stared at her, speechless.

"I'll take that as a no," Cerys replied. "Run!"

She seized Anwen's hand and dragged her away.

"We're upside down!" said Anwen.

"It's just a glamour spell, stupid," said Cerys. "But I can't hold it for long, so we need to get out of here."

"What about the doors?" said Anwen. As far as she could tell, the doors were in front of them, but thirty feet in the air, and upside down.

"Don't trust what you see," Cerys replied, at which point they both ran face-first into something solid and invisible that knocked them both onto their backsides.

With Cerys's concentration broken, the glamour spell dissolved, and the ballroom instantly righted itself, leaving them sprawled at the feet of one of the china dolls.

"I forgot these stupid things were here," said Cerys.

Anwen looked back as they picked themselves up. Stillpike was reeling toward them, clearly still disoriented, but he had the saber in his hand again, and a look of pure fury in his eyes.

"Cerys Powell!" he bellowed. "You brat! I'll fillet you too."

Cerys turned toward the exit, only for Anwen to pull her back.

"We need his guitar," said Anwen. "It's the key to everything."

"Why didn't you tell me sooner?" Cerys looked around frantically. "Quick, this way." She pulled Anwen behind the voluminous crinoline skirts of one of the dancers.

"Do you think I'm blind?" said Stillpike, making toward them.

Anwen squeezed Cerys's hand as she heard his footsteps approach. "We can't stay here."

"I know," Cerys replied. Then, to Anwen's horror, Cerys shoved her out from behind the doll, right into Stillpike's path.

She froze, but instead of the swift death blow she had expected, Stillpike paused and looked around in confusion.

Another Anwen had stepped into view from behind the next pair of dolls.

"A clever trick," said Stillpike. "But I'll just run you both through."

Before he had even finished speaking, a third Anwen appeared, and then a fourth, fifth, and sixth. Within seconds, he was surrounded.

"Go!" shouted Cerys.

Anwen ran for the throne. As she did so, the other Anwens scattered, sprinting in all directions. Stillpike bellowed with rage and swung the saber wildly at them. He missed Anwen's head by inches, but immediately pivoted to slash at one of the copies. The blade passed through it like smoke.

Anwen reached the throne, and had just seized the guitar when she heard Cerys cry out in pain. Her duplicates evaporated into nothingness, leaving only the dolls, and the chilling sight of Stillpike standing over a fallen Cerys, who was bleeding from a wound on her arm.

"You always were a snot-nosed little pain," Stillpike said as Cerys looked fearfully up at him. "No more tricks for you."

Anwen didn't think. She sprinted toward Stillpike as he raised his saber for the killing blow, and she brought the guitar down on his head like a club. "Leave my friend alone!"

The guitar connected with a hollow *thunk*, and Stillpike went rigid. His eyes crossed, and he wobbled on the spot for a moment, then keeled over backward.

He landed beside Cerys, who was red faced and tearful. "You took your time," she gasped.

"You're welcome," said Anwen. "Are you all right?"

Cerys put her hand to the wound and winced. "Of course not. Look what he did to my new jacket!"

Anwen laughed. "You *and* the jacket just need a few stitches," she said. "Let's go." She helped her friend up, and they limped toward the doors together.

"What are you doing here, anyway?" Anwen asked.

"I made your grandma send Colin back up through the thin place to fetch Archimboldo, so he could give me a ride," Cerys replied. "He took me to the roof, and I followed the music from there. I thought you might need my help."

Anwen pulled Cerys a little closer. "Thanks."

They both paused in the doorway, and looked back at Stillpike's supine form.

"What about him?" asked Cerys.

"He'll be out for a while," Anwen replied. "The Maestro was right—Thibault's guitar was magic, and Stillpike was supplying all the music. He and Marcus arranged the murder between them."

Cerys's face fell. "Not Marcus!" she said. "I liked him."

"So did I," said Anwen. "But with any luck, he'll be under arrest by now."

They were halfway down the stairs when Fame Hall started to shake. The chandeliers danced, and dust pattered like rain against the roof.

"What's happening?" said Cerys.

A sound like thunder resolved into the pounding of giant footsteps. Lots and lots of giant footsteps, approaching at a run.

"Stillpike!"

Anwen's blood ran cold. It was Marcus's voice.

He crashed to his knees outside Fame Hall, yanked the front of the dollhouse open, and thrust his face inside.

"We have to go, Stillpike!" he said, his ragged breath filling the house. "They're coming!"

He saw the girls cowering against the stairs, and the guitar in Anwen's hand. "You two!" he said. "You've ruined everything!"

With nowhere to run, Anwen and Cerys clung to each other as the shadow of his enormous hand fell over them.

29

Restoration

The rumble of footsteps hadn't stopped, and before Marcus could close his fingers around Anwen and Cerys, another pair of hands seized him by the shoulders and dragged him backward. Suddenly, the attic was full of people—the Captain, holding a struggling Marcus; an entire squad of palace guards; the Maestro; and, to Anwen's absolute joy, Tonino, looking shaken but unharmed.

The page boy's face lit up at the sight of them, and he pushed his way to Fame Hall and offered them his hat to climb into.

"You're all right!" said Anwen.

"Yes," he said, beaming down at them. "Although I'll be glad never to see another wardrobe."

Cerys quickly applied her amplification spell. "What happened?" she asked. "I feel like I missed all the good bits."

"The Maestro found me just in time," said Tonino. "Then all these guards burst in and arrested him, until I told them about everything that had happened. So then they tried to arrest Marcus, but he made a break for it, and here we are."

The Maestro appeared over his shoulder. "I'm happy to have done my part," he said. He spotted Stillpike's guitar in her hands, and leaned in until his nose almost knocked her over. "Is that . . . ?" he asked.

"The guitar that controls Thibault's?" she answered. "Yes. You'd better take it." She placed it on the tip of his outstretched finger.

"I shall guard it with my life," he said, but almost dropped it as Marcus struggled to break free of the Captain's grip.

"Cato, you have to let me try again. I was so close!"

The Captain's expression was thunderous as he secured Marcus's hands behind his back. "Close to what?"

"Success! Stardom! Everything we ever dreamed of."

The Captain shook his head sadly. "I never dreamed of anything like this," he said.

A short while later, Anwen, Cerys, the Maestro, and Tonino joined the rest of the royal court in the throne room. For the first time since their arrival, Anwen noticed a buzz of optimism in the air, although silence fell as Queen Flavia retook her place on the throne.

"It's certainly been quite a day," Flavia said, smoothing out the folds of her dress. "Arrested, deposed, and acquitted in the space of a day." Her eyes traveled around the assembly. "Captain, your report, please."

The Captain bowed. "We've apprehended those responsible for your brother's murder, Your Majesty, and for the attacks on the Maestro and the Chamberlain. Furthermore, both the enchanted guitars have been recovered."

He motioned to the Maestro, who approached the throne, went down on one knee, and extended his hand. Stillpike's guitar rested in the center of his palm, looking for all the world like a doll's accessory.

"How odd to think that something so small could have such an enormous influence," said Flavia. "But I still don't understand why these guitars exist at all."

The Maestro cleared his throat. "Allow me to enlighten you, Your Majesty, for I have plumbed the depths of knowledge in search of—"

"A summary will do, thank you," she interrupted.

He bowed. "The guitars are relics of an age long before the Beanstalk Wars. Human music was very popular in our kingdom at that time, but of course the instruments and voices were too small for giant ears to hear. The twinned guitars were created by human magicians as a means to perform music on a grander scale, and human minstrels sometimes toured our kingdom with a giant partner to handle the mimic guitar. Think of it as a novelty double act. It was a short-lived phenomenon, and from a strictly academic standpoint I'm thrilled to have seen it resurrected."

"Lucky you," said Flavia flatly. "But you raise a thorny question. This crime spans two worlds, so how are we to settle it?" She drummed her fingers on the throne's armrest and raised a questioning eyebrow at Anwen and Cerys.

"What about a joint trial, Your Majesty?" said Anwen.

Flavia's other eyebrow rose to match the first. "Both worlds working together? That hasn't happened in more than a century."

"Excuse me!" Cerys puffed her chest out. "We've managed pretty well over the last couple of days."

Flavia smiled. "Point taken," she said. "Captain? Bring in the prisoners. I would like to speak with them."

At a signal from the Captain, four guards entered. Marcus was shackled between two of them, his head bowed, while the other two carried an antique birdcage on a stand, salvaged from the junk in the attic. Stillpike was inside it, clutching the bars.

"Well?" said Flavia, regarding them both with cold disdain. "Do you have anything to say for yourselves?"

Marcus mumbled something under his breath.

"Speak up," said Flavia.

"I said, your brother was a fraud," Marcus replied. "He didn't deserve any of the praise he got."

There was silence from the court, as thick as fog.

"You're right, he didn't," said Flavia. "But neither do you. And he didn't kill anyone in the process."

"Wouldn't you kill for the thing you wanted most?" he asked, before turning to the Captain. "Cato, tell her! We were going to have everything we wanted until the Maestro turned us down."

The Captain shook his head, his expression a mixture of horror and pity. "Marcus, we were kids. We just weren't good enough. I'm glad we tried, but failing the audition was the best thing that ever happened to me. I found a better dream. I wish you'd done the same."

Marcus hung his head again, and fell silent.

"And what about you, minstrel?" Flavia asked Stillpike.

"I wanted nothing more than wealth and comfort," he said. "And I would have gotten away with it, if it wasn't for those meddling kids and their giant pigeon."

With a dismissive wave, Flavia had the guards remove Marcus and Stillpike. "As for you two," she said, turning to Anwen and Cerys, "I have a lot to thank you both for. Your tenacity deserves a reward. Name it, and it's yours."

Cerys bolted upright. "More gold?"

Anwen elbowed her hard. "We've got plenty of gold, Your Majesty. But perhaps you could keep the cats in the kitchen, and put some food in the attic for the mice each night, where it's safer. They'd really appreciate it."

Flavia sat back in surprise. "Is that really all?"

Anwen reflected for a moment. "Oh, could you add some pigeons to the murals in the nursery? Their plumage is actually quite beautiful, if you look closely."

"Mice," said Flavia. "And pigeons."

"Yes, please," said Anwen. "We couldn't have done it without them."

"Consider it done," said Flavia. "Chamberlain? Are you well enough to see to it?"

Anwen turned in surprise as the courtiers parted for the Chamberlain, who shuffled awkwardly to the throne. His head was bandaged, and he swayed a little on his feet but still managed a respectful bow.

"No, Your Majesty," he said. "In fact, I'm here to tender my resignation."

Everyone gasped, including Flavia.

"Who will maintain protocol without you?" she asked.

"I don't care," he replied. "This job is killing me, in more ways than one. So, I'm finished."

Flavia looked chastened. "What will you do instead?"

"I don't know." He laughed. "For the first time in my life, I have no idea. Isn't that wonderful? I might retire to a cabin in the woods, or pitch a tent on a beach somewhere. I could take up painting, or collect seashells, or run naked through the streets."

"That last one's illegal," said the Captain. The rest of the court nodded vigorously.

"My point is, palace protocol is someone else's problem now," said the Chamberlain. "You can make it up as you go along, for all I care."

Everyone watched Flavia expectantly. "Perhaps it *is* time for a fresh set of ideas," she mused. "How would you like a promotion, Tonino?"

"Me?" he said. "But I can't! Can I?"

Flavia shrugged. "You're honest and dependable, and you're clearly not afraid to stand up to me. I'll make sure you're never given *too* much to do, but I will need someone to liaise with the Land Below in the months ahead." She smiled. "You seem to have the diplomatic touch."

Tonino rose up onto the balls of his feet with excitement. "Would I get to go and visit?"

“Maybe,” said Flavia. “The least our worlds can do is start talking to each other again.”

Tonino looked down at Anwen and Cerys. “What do you think?” he said. “Should I take it?”

“Yes!” they chorused.

“All right,” he said, grinning hugely. “I accept, Your Majesty!”

“Splendid,” said Flavia. “Your first order of business—get these young ladies home.”

30

Parting Ways

Anwen and Cerys stood together in the remains of Old Stump, watching the giant basket withdraw into the sky. When it was little more than a speck in the blue distance, it vanished completely.

"We're finally all back on solid ground together," said Eira, putting an arm around Anwen. "No more running off?"

"I'm not going anywhere." Anwen leaned into the hug but snapped upright again when the ground began to tremble. Cerys felt it too, and they exchanged an anxious look.

"What is it now?" said Cerys.

The tremor resolved into the tramp of many feet, and a battalion of soldiers came into view, advancing along the western road at a quick march. Their commanding officer, mounted on horseback, brought them to a crashing halt at the field hospital.

"Lieutenant Colonel Larsson of the Third Battalion, Capital Regiment," he said, dismounting. "The First Minister dispatched us to counter the attack from the Sky Kingdom."

"Oh?" Eira raised an eyebrow. "What attack would that be?"

"Er . . ." The Lieutenant Colonel drew his sword and waved it in the general direction of the ruined village. "This one?" He looked to his men for support, but they seemed as nonplussed as he was. He turned back to Eira. "Was this an attack?"

Eira clapped him on the shoulder. "Tell your men to stand down, I'll put the kettle on, and we can have a nice long chat about it," she said. She steered the Lieutenant Colonel toward her cottage.

Anwen was just thinking that a cup of tea sounded like the best idea in the world when the sound of galloping hooves and rattling wheels approached. Seconds later, a bright red stagecoach, pulled by two sweating horses, raced into the rubble-strewn patch where Old Stump had once stood. The driver pulled back on the reins and brought the coach to a stop. At the same time, the coach's door flew open and a man leapt out, grinning widely. It was Cerys's father.

"Sweetheart!" He ran and grabbed Cerys by the shoulders. "It's the mail coach!"

"Yes, Dad, I can see that," she replied. "What about it?"

"It was delayed once word about the giant got

out, but now it's leaving," he said. "You don't want to miss your seat."

"Now?" she said. "But I've only just gotten back."

"And you're already late for the Academy," her father said. "Your mum and I have packed your luggage for you."

"But Dad, I—"

He steered her toward the open carriage door. "You're going to make us so proud, sweetheart. All your hard work is about to pay off."

She dug her heels into the ground and brought them both to an abrupt stop. "Dad, please!"

Her father looked surprised. "What's wrong?"

"I just . . . I just want to say goodbye to Anwen first."

Anwen tensed as Cerys made her way awkwardly over.

"I suppose this is it, then," said Cerys.

"Yeah," Anwen replied. "I suppose so." She wasn't sure what to do with her hands, so she stuffed them into her dress pockets. "Thanks for coming back for me in the attic."

"That's okay," said Cerys. "I'm sorry for all the things I said before."

"No, I deserved it," said Anwen. "And you deserve this. You're the best magic user I've ever met. I just hated the idea of being second best."

"I should never have tried to make you think you were," said Cerys. "Your magic's really powerful too. I'm sure you could get into the Academy next year, if you apply again."

Anwen looked around at the wildflowers in the fields and the birds riding the air currents high above them. She saw the crowd of soldiers, now milling around aimlessly while Eira talked the Lieutenant Colonel's ear off. "Actually, I'd like to stay here and finish my apprenticeship. There's a lot more to being a Meadow Witch than I realized, and I have a feeling Old Stump is going to be busier than ever soon."

She was surprised to see the look of disappointment on Cerys's face.

"Maybe you could just come and visit?" said Cerys.

"I'd like that."

Cerys smiled. "Me too."

Anwen pulled her into a hug, then walked with her to the waiting mail coach. The horses stamped impatiently.

"Give her a smooth ride, please," Anwen whispered to them. "And get her there safely."

The horses snorted and flicked their ears.

"So what if I *am* telling you how to do your jobs?" she said. "Honestly, you horses are such snobs. I never have this problem with donkeys."

The driver cracked his whip and the coach rolled forward. Anwen joined Cerys's parents and waved until it was out of sight on the western road. Cerys's father dabbed at his eyes with a handkerchief.

"My little star."

Anwen took his hand. "She'll do brilliantly, Mr. Powell. I promise."

Half an hour later, the Lieutenant Colonel emerged from Eira's cottage looking rather shell-shocked, rolling a gold coin the size of a tabletop beside him. Eira waved him off from the doorstep.

"Lovely chatting with you, Arthur," she said. "You and your men have a safe trip back, and don't be afraid to use that poultice I gave you if your bunions start acting up again."

He nodded distractedly and wheeled the huge coin toward his waiting men. "Pack up your kit, lads, we're heading home. And for goodness' sake, someone help me carry this thing."

Anwen joined Eira on the doorstep and watched the soldiers lash the coin to one of their equipment wagons. "That was quick," she said. "I expected more shouting."

"Luckily for us, he's quite a sensible young man,"

said Eira. "Once I convinced him there wasn't a fight to be had, he became quite amenable. He's taking the coin back to the First Minister as a sign of goodwill, and a lot of people in expensive suits will be here to open diplomatic relations with the Sky Kingdom next week. We've got an interesting time ahead of us."

Anwen looked out over the remains of the village that had been the stage for her whole life up until two days ago, and realized she would never see it quite as it had been ever again. It would have to change, and that was all right—it was making room for a bigger world, with bigger people in it. Much bigger. She had no idea what her place in that world would be yet, but that was a question that could wait until tomorrow.

"Is there still tea in the pot?" she asked Eira.

"When is there not?"

Anwen laughed. "Of course. I should know that by now."

"You obviously haven't been paying attention," said Eira. "Time to refresh your memory."

They went inside and shut the door behind them.

Acknowledgments

This book was born in the depths of the Covid lockdown, and for a while I was certain I would never finish it. That I have is thanks to the following wonderful people: Clare Charles and Helen Clifford of community arts project Made in Roath, for the generous loan of a studio space, and my wonderful wife, Anna, for arranging it.

Pippa and Nina Andrews for their feedback on the opening chapters of the very first draft. Robin Stevens, for her encouragement and insights into her plotting process. Aurelien, for solving Marcus's backstory in one fell swoop: "What if he was in a band?"

My agent, Gemma Cooper, who steered both me and this book through some very choppy post-Covid waters. And finally, my brilliant editors: Foyinsi Adegbonmire at Feiwel & Friends and Sarah Stewart at Usborne. Thank you for helping me shape this book into what it finally became.

Thank you for reading this Feiwel & Friends book.

The friends who made

THE BEANSTALK MURDER

possible are:

Jean Feiwel, Publisher
Liz Szabla, VP, Associate Publisher
Rich Deas, Senior Creative Director
Anna Roberto, Executive Editor
Holly West, Senior Editor
Kat Brzozowski, Senior Editor
Dawn Ryan, Executive Managing Editor
Kim Waymer, Senior Production Manager
Emily Settle, Editor
Rachel Diebel, Editor
Foyinsi Adegbonmire, Editor
Brittany Groves, Assistant Editor
Megan Sayre, Junior Designer
Ilana Worrell, Senior Production Editor
Kelly Markus, Production Editorial Assistant

Follow us on Facebook or visit us online at mackids.com.

Our books are friends for life.

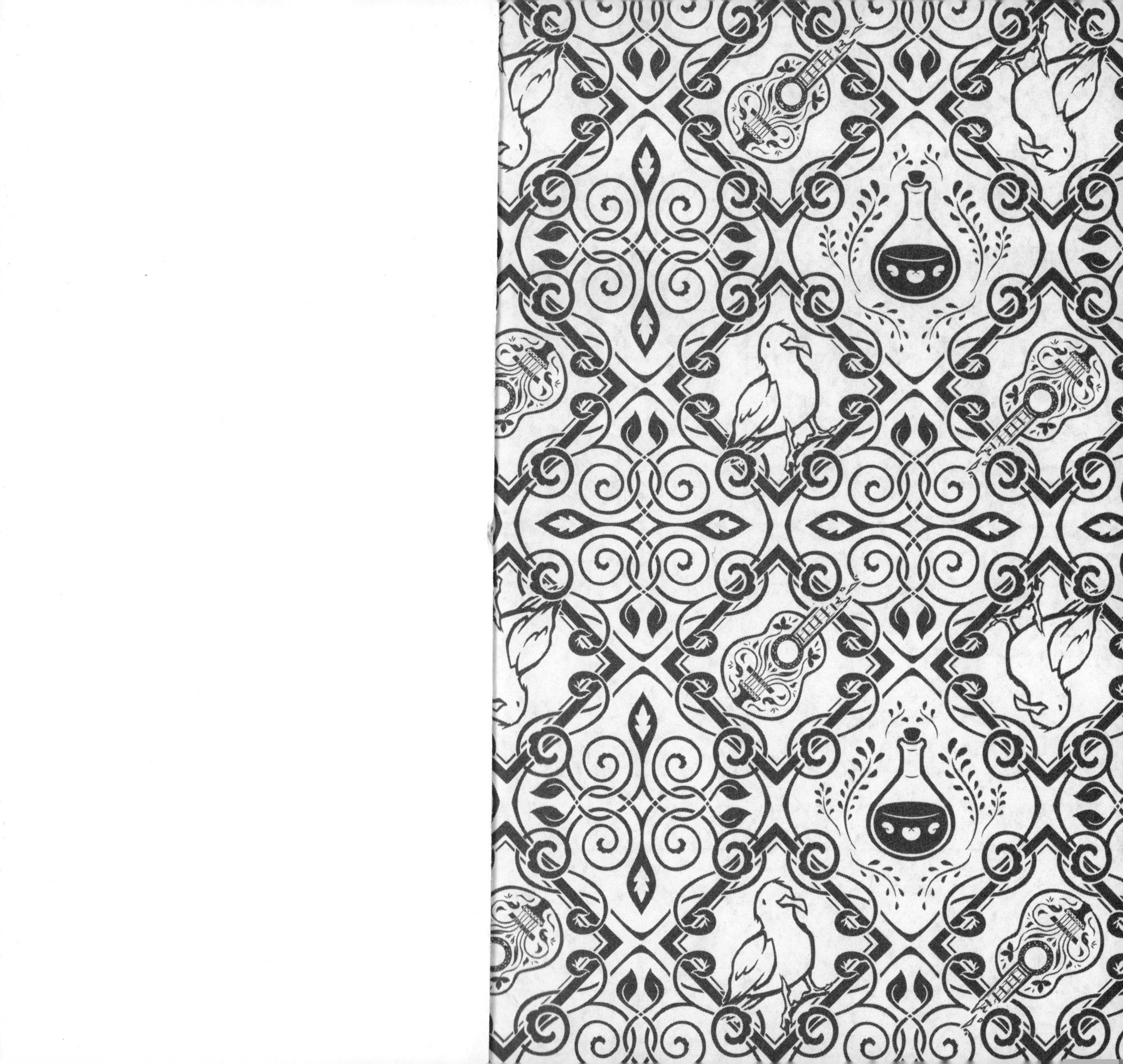